"Why did you marry me, Ryan?"

Meredith's question was abrupt. Nerves, anger and hurt all fused into one within her. She saw the alert look in his eyes, but he was cool, and apparently still in fine good humor.

"It seemed like a good idea at the time," he drawled.

Meredith could see nothing to be good-humored about and silently stared at him. To his credit, though, Ryan was not a man who would look away from trouble. And after waiting a minute longer for her to follow up—if she was going to—he took the initiative from her.

"I refuse to begin our marriage with you going into a fit of sulks over some imagined slight," he told her bluntly. "So out with it—let's have it all."

Jessica Steele first tried her hand at writing romance novels at her husband's encouragement two years after they were married. She fondly remembers the day her first novel was accepted for publication. "Peter mopped me up, and neither of us cooked that night," she recalls. "We went out to dinner." She and her husband live in a hundred-year-old cottage in Worcestershire, and they've traveled to many fascinating places—such as China, Japan, Mexico and Denmark—that make wonderful settings for her books.

Farewell to Love

Jessica Steele

Harlequin Books

TORONTO • NEW YORK • LONDON
AMSTERDAM • PARIS • SYDNEY • HAMBURG
STOCKHOLM • ATHENS • TOKYO • MILAN

Original hardcover edition published in 1989
by Mills & Boon Limited

ISBN 0-373-03041-X

Harlequin Romance first edition March 1990

CHAPTER ONE

WAS ever a girl so happy? Meredith caught sight of herself in her full-length bedroom mirror, and could not help smiling at the young woman in bridal attire who smiled back. Today was her wedding day. Today, only a few hours ago in fact, she had married Ryan Carlisle.

A sudden movement drew her attention to her great-aunt Evelyn, who had come to her room with her for the traditional purpose of helping her to get changed into her going-away outfit. Not that she and Ryan were going away, for he was a very busy man, and, with everything happening so fast, it just was not convenient for him to leave his business at present.

'Are you all right, Aunty?' Meredith queried, and re-alised that the shimmer of tears in her great-aunt's eyes came only from her loving thoughts of the moment.

'I've never seen you look so happy,' Miss Evelyn Simmons sighed softly.

'I've never felt so happy,' Meredith replied gently—though she quickly qualified that lest she should have unintentionally wounded her great-aunt. 'Not that I haven't been happy living here with you and Uncle Porter all these years, and with Grandfather too, when he was alive,' she smiled.

'I know, dear, I know,' Evelyn Simmons said sweetly. Though her misty-eyed look had vanished when, being realistic for one of the very few times in her life, she added, 'Your grandfather would have been proud of you this day.'

Meredith, having lived in the Simmons household from the age of five, knew exactly what she meant. Grandfather Simmons had been a hard man, a man who worshipped money and a man, it seemed, who had been entirely without sentiment. Had he been alive today he would have been more proud to have witnessed that she had married herself to a man of some wealth than that she was happy to marry the man she loved—and the man who loved her. Not that Ryan had ever said he loved her, but Meredith knew he did—why else would he have married her?

She turned her back on a small moment of disquiet and, smiling at her great-aunt, observed signs of tiredness in the face of her dear old-fashioned seventy-nine-year-old relative. 'I can manage on my own, Aunty,' she told her quickly, and, indicating the small bedroom chair, suggested, 'Why not rest for a few minutes?'

Miss Simmons began to waver, but it was soon apparent that she was more concerned over her brother, her junior by two years.

'Tessa should have been here to help you,' she stated, bringing out Tessa's name somewhat begrudgingly, for she had never approved of the way Meredith's friend had gone to live with Duncan Smith without benefit of a marriage ceremony. 'If you're sure you can manage, though, I shouldn't at all mind going to keep an eye on Porter. He's not at all used to strong drink, but I'm sure I saw him helping himself to a second glass of champagne. What with his heart and...'

'You go, darling,' Meredith urged, having previously explained why Tessa could not be with them at such short notice. Feeling saddened for a moment when she thought of how tragically Duncan had died eighteen months ago, Meredith placed an arm about her great-aunt's shoulders and walked to the door with her. 'You worry too much about that brother of yours,' she told her, aware herself that her great-uncle Porter might, in his seventy-seventh year, have something of a tired heart, but also aware that he was not above playing on his 'heart condition' when he wanted his own way about something. 'I'll be down as soon as I've changed,' she smiled to her aunt.

Meredith's head was filled with thoughts of Ryan Carlisle once her aunt had gone. 'Ryan Carlisle, my husband,' she breathed out loud. 'Meredith Carlisle,' she added, savouring the name; already Meredith Maybry, her maiden name, seemed light years away. Suddenly Meredith gave a self-conscious laugh, and hastened to her wardrobe to extract her going-away suit.

The smile was back on her face as she stepped from her white wedding dress. The wedding arrangements had been made so fast that there had been no time to shop for a wedding gown, but she was glad now that Aunt Evelyn had insisted she find time.

Meredith was brimful of happiness as she donned the blue suit which brought out the bright blue colour of her eyes. The new suit had been another 'must' that her aunt had insisted upon. Even when Meredith had told her that she did not really need a going-away outfit, since with no time for a honeymoon she was only taking a half-hour journey across London to Ryan's apartment, her aunt had again insisted.

'I'm not having the neighbours seeing you leave home in something they've seen you wearing a dozen times before,' Evelyn Simmons had said firmly—at which Meredith had hardly been able to prevent herself from laughing.

'But we only have one near neighbour!' she had protested. Mrs Peplow, next door, was the same seventy-nine years as her great-aunt, and was a lady Meredith had known since she had come to live with her mother's kin, seventeen years ago. 'And besides being your friend, she's more family than...'

'Lilian Peplow may be my very good friend as well as our neighbour,' her aunt interrupted, 'but that's by no means any excuse for allowing our standards to drop.' Rather than upset her dear aunt, Meredith had somehow found the time to do as she wished.

Once that suit she had purchased was neatly zipped up and buttoned, however, Meredith was glad that her aunt had insisted the way she had. For suddenly she was feeling slightly nervous and on checking her appearance she saw, without conceit, that the blue of the two-piece, as well as enhancing the colour of her bright blue eyes, seemed to give an added something to the creamy complexion of her skin, and to the shining blonde of her hair.

With a mixture of emotions bombarding her at the thought of going down the stairs to join her new husband, and of leaving the home she had known for most of her life, Meredith needed a minute or two in which to collect herself. The man she had that day married was a man of some sophistication and, at pains not to seem unsophisticated to him, she seated herself in the chair which she had earlier suggested her great-aunt might rest in, deciding that a few more minutes spent in calming herself would do no harm.

Though, as she began to feel more calm about the one issue, she began to have qualms about leaving her elderly relatives. Suddenly, now that the time had come to leave her home, and them with it, she was starting to feel guilty that she had ever for a single moment experienced an occasional if firmly held down urge to do something different with her life. More frequently of late, she owned, up until the time she had met Ryan, she had known an out-of-character restlessness within herself—a restlessness that had pushed her to want to leave home. But to leave the home she shared with her aged great-aunt and great-uncle had been out of the question then.

Not that she had never been away from home. She had—once. That had been the dreadful time a year and a half ago when Tessa's Duncan had died. She had gone straight away to be with her friend in Derbyshire and to be what help she could. But she had only been able to stay a week, because Great-Uncle Porter had suffered one of his 'heart turns' and she had been summoned urgently home again.

Meredith sometimes thought that her great-uncle must have the most remarkable heart, for countless were the times when he would have them all believe that he was at death's door, but each time he recovered.

It was because of him, and his dicky heart, that she did not have a permanent job. Her thoughts drifted back to how, on the death of her parents in an accident when she was five years old, she had been taken to live with the two brothers and one sister—her mother's only relatives. As she had been brought up most strictly, however, with every word her grandfather uttered being law, it was not until after his death when Meredith was fifteen that there had been any lessening of the stern atmosphere. Her uncle Porter was inclined to be a shade domineering at times, it was true, and was growing more like his brother Ogden every day, but both he and Aunt Evelyn were kind to her, and in due time had even allowed her to go to art college with her great friend Tessa Wallace—something which would have been unthinkable in her grandfather's day.

Tessa was a born artist, while Meredith accepted that she merely had flair. She had worked hard, though, and, while Tessa went on to specialise in painting landscapes, she had gone on to specialise in design.

But, for all their training and talent, Tessa found it difficult to scrape a living out of painting landscapes and she moved to Little Haversham, on the outskirts of Derby, with Duncan, while Meredith eagerly sought a job in which she could use her training.

Her spirit was undaunted when no job seemed available, and she applied for a job as a window-dresser, to discover that window-dressing was where her real talent lay.

Unfortunately, while Uncle Porter had made no objection to her going to art school, it appeared that he had a good many objections to her going out to work. They were not wealthy by any means, and lived modestly on money left to them by Meredith's great-grandfather—money which might have been a vast sum once, but which over the years had dwindled and dwindled in value. But just the same, when Meredith was called home twice in her first week at her window-dressing job because Uncle Porter was having pains in his chest, and three times in her second week for the same reason, she felt that she could do no other than give in her notice before her employers gave it for her.

When the next two window-dressing jobs she applied for and got had to be given up because of her great-uncle's repeated bouts of illness, Meredith was forced to give way. Clearly Uncle Porter frowned on her going out to work. All she was doing by attempting to carve out a career in the window-dressing world was getting herself a bad name for being unreliable.

For once, though, Meredith experienced a strange feeling of rebellion and, acting on that feeling, she had put her name down on a register for temporary work, should any become available. Which—her eyes grew dreamy—was how she had come to meet Ryan.

The agency had rung her a week before that fateful day. Montgomery's, a mammoth new store which had been under construction for an age, was at last almost ready for the grand opening day. Everyone was frantically busy, because with a top-class celebrity booked, nothing could halt the store's being opened next Friday— nothing at all. A large hiccup had occurred in the build-up to next Friday, though, in that half the preparation staff had suddenly gone down with some tummy bug and, although there were dark mutterings about canteen food, dark mutterings were not going to get the job completed in time.

'Can you help?' implored the harassed woman from the agency, having had to find a good many workers from window-cleaners to carpet fitters.

'Do you think I'm good enough?' Meredith asked doubtfully. Montgomery's were an upmarket firm and, thanks to Uncle Porter, she felt she could in no way be called professional yet.

'You won't be working on your own,' the woman assured her. 'And I can promise you that any pair of artistic hands and artistic eyes will be more than welcome.'

'Then I'll be pleased to do it,' Meredith told her.

She had been too. She had put up with Uncle Porter's sour looks when she had told him where she was going, and she'd had a quiet word with Mrs Key, their daily help, and asked her to keep an eye on him for her. And, after a back-breaking week, she was quite pleased with her window-dressing efforts.

So, too, was the chief window-dresser, for he had thanked her very much, and said that she must come along to the store's opening the next day.

Almost, she had not gone. Had it not been for the Shakespearean actor who had been engaged to open the store, and whom Meredith had admired for his acting when she had seen him on TV, then she would not have gone. Nor would she have ever met Ryan Carlisle. Not that she was introduced to him, for as far as she could make out, when on Friday morning she stood tucked in with the rest of the staff, no one as lowly as a window-dresser had been invited to be part of the VIP party.

At that point, though, she had no inclination whatsoever to rub shoulders with the top brass. But although she, along with nearly everyone else, was eager for a sight of the Shakespearean actor, suddenly she lost all interest in him. 'That's Mr Montgomery,' she heard someone say. 'The white-haired, sprightly-looking chap.'

All eyes turned to see Mr Montgomery, and as Meredith took in the impeccably dressed white-haired man, her glance strayed to the tall, well-to-do-looking man standing talking to him. Her glance stayed on him. Indeed, she felt incapable of taking her eyes off him. And suddenly her heart was beating faster so that she almost had to gasp for breath. For, just as suddenly, though she had never seen the dark-haired man in her life before, though she did not so much as know his name, Meredith knew that she was in love. Feeling unable to take her eyes from him, Meredith, with a fast-beating heart, took in the fact that he appeared to be somewhere in his mid-thirties, that he was as impeccably dressed as his companion, and also that she had not a hope in the world that a man of his sophistication would ever notice, far less fall in love with, anyone such as her.

She managed to take her eyes from him as the opening ceremony got under way, and gave herself the sternest lecture on being such a crazy idiot as to imagine that she had fallen in love at first sight, and with a complete stranger. But she only had to flick a glance at him, as she did every now and again while the actor cut a wide ribbon and made a speech and then Mr Montgomery made a speech, to feel that same never-before-known emotion.

'Are you coming, Meredith?' another window-dresser asked, making her realise that the opening ceremony was over.

'I—er—think I left something in the staff-room,' she quickly and equally crazily invented.

On reflection, though, Meredith decided that perhaps her invention of the moment was not so crazy after all. For 'with all hands on deck', so to speak, now that the general public had been let into the store, it was pretty near guaranteed that the staff-room was empty.

Realising that she needed to be alone to try and get herself together from the shattering experience she had just undergone, Meredith said a hurried farewell to her window-dresser acquaintance and went as hurriedly to the staff-room.

Much good did it do her, though. Because although the staff-room was empty, and there was no one there to interrupt her train of thought, Meredith still didn't know quite what had hit her half an hour later.

It was ridiculous, she reiterated, trying to summon up the saner part of her. Why, she didn't even know the man's name!

She was still in the staff-room when, five minutes later, one of the salesgirls dashed in. 'It's bedlam out there!'

she told her, changing her high heels for a more practical pair of shoes and dashing out again.

Guessing that other staff would dive in from time to time and that she could not hope to have the staff-room to herself for much longer, Meredith prepared to go home. What was the point of staying, anyway? she thought as she made for the staff lift. She wasn't going to see him again, she wasn't going to speak to him ever, and, since there seemed to be something very active about him, he had probably left the Montgomery building already and, for all she knew, was at some other opening ceremony.

She had reached the staff lift and had just pressed the call button, though, when, to prove that he was not at some other opening, and that indeed he had not even left the building, the man she had so instantly given her heart to came and stood next to her. Suddenly, as her heart set up a tremendous clamouring, Meredith's legs at the same time felt so weak that she had no idea how she was going to step forward into the lift when it came. For, grateful for the smallest crumb, she saw that it seemed she was going to travel down in the lift with him—just the two of them!

Striving hard to keep her sense of mental balance, for this man had the oddest effect on her, she guessed that he had chosen to take the staff lift out of the store as the quickest route.

The lift arrived and, ready to admire the least thing about him, Meredith admired the courteous way he waited a second for her to precede him into the lift. 'Thank you,' she murmured politely. She admired him more when, with his finger over the ground-floor button, he looked at her enquiringly.

She nodded, and had the bonus as he went to turn from her of catching sight of the name-tag which store security had insisted that every visitor, bar customers, wore before the start of proceedings that morning, and which, now he was leaving the store, he had started to remove. Not, though, before she had read, 'R. Carlisle, Carlisle Electronics'.

He had pocketed the name-tab and the lift had started to descend when, in sheer desperation, acting totally unlike the normally reserved person she believed herself to be, Meredith heard her own voice suddenly blurt out, 'I have interests in the electrical field too!'

'It's—a small world,' he replied smoothly, and Meredith knew, just *knew*, that he was thinking, 'Liar'.

'I truly have,' she said earnestly, and became enormously aware that she was going to have to make a bigger fool of herself than ever. Because she felt obliged to confess, 'My father left me thousands and thousands of shares in Burgess Electrical.' Standing that close to him, she could not miss the sudden surprised look he gave her; and, grabbing at what pride she could, she got in first before he could beat her to it. Feeling even more stupid, she had to add, 'But, as you no doubt know, Burgess Electrical shares aren't worth the paper they're written on.'

The gods were merciful to her when at that point the lift reached the ground floor. R. Carlisle of Carlisle Electronics was still looking at her as though it was not every day that some lying window-dresser accosted him in a staff lift. When the lift doors opened, this time wanting to be as far away from him as she could, Meredith shot through them as though her heels were on fire.

The next afternoon she was in the sitting-room with her great-aunt and great-uncle and was still going through agonies about her actions yesterday. Oh, where, she inwardly mourned, had her customary reserve been then?

She only realised that she had sighed when her aunt looked at her. But just then the phone, which was always placed on a table near to Uncle Porter, rang.

He picked it up. 'Hello,' he said, sounding a trifle grumpy as he did sometimes. There followed a few moments' pause, during which Meredith started to wonder why he should begin to look as grumpy as he sounded, and then she heard him ask bluntly, 'Who wants her?' He looked more disgruntled than ever when, to her absolute stupefaction, he held the phone out to her and said, 'It's for you! He says his name's Ryan Carlisle.'

'For...' Meredith said croakily, and even while her mind quickly translated the 'R. Carlisle' she had been thinking about for the past twenty-four hours into Ryan Carlisle, she just could not credit that he could be on the other end of the phone! But her great-uncle was starting to look cross that she was not coming to take the phone from him and, because she realised that her thinking had been all haywire since yesterday anyway, so that it was nothing but plain coincidence that a Ryan Carlisle was ringing her about something, she went and took the phone from her uncle. 'Hello,' she said.

'Hello, Meredith,' said an absolutely sensational voice which she just knew belonged to none other than the man who, unbeknown to him, had kept her sleepless last night. 'We met yesterday, in a lift,' he reminded her, when there was absolutely no need. 'After the Montgomery store opening,' he added.

'Oh—yes, I—I remember,' Meredith replied, fighting with all she had to keep her voice even.

'I wonder if you're free to have dinner with me to-night,' he queried.

Scarcely believing that she was hearing what she was hearing, Meredith knew that if she did happen to have a previous engagement—which she didn't—she would have broken it. 'I—should like that,' she told him honestly.

'I'll call for you at seven-thirty,' he told her, and rang off.

Which, had he but known it, left Meredith in a flat spin. Though before she could deal with her own doubts and fears she had to deal with her relatives.

'Who was that?' Uncle Porter demanded to know.

'A—friend,' Meredith told him. 'He's taking me out to dinner tonight.'

'Why, that's lovely, my dear,' said her aunt, as if she had only just realised that her great-niece seldom if ever went out in the evening.

'What about *my* dinner?' Uncle Porter questioned, at his demanding worst.

'You're not helpless, Porter,' his sister told him shortly. 'Besides, Meredith deserves a night out with her young man. And anyway, I helped her prepare a casserole for dinner this morning, so you won't starve if...'

'Her young man!' Porter exploded, forgetting his stomach as he exclaimed more or less what Meredith had been thinking.

Her young man, she thought when later up in her room she looked with dissatisfaction at the contents of a wardrobe with which yesterday she had been perfectly satisfied. Oh, what was she going to wear?

By seven-fifteen, having changed several times from one dress to another, she was finally ready. Attired in a smart black dress which was neither too revealing nor too modest, she sat in her room and went through agony after agony as she wondered—had he been serious?

He had sounded serious, she remembered, not wanting to start believing that because she had been so idiotic as to tell him of those worthless shares yesterday he thought—having recovered from being so accosted—that he would play a little game with her.

It couldn't be some game he was playing to teach her not to try and get into conversation with unknown men in a lift, could it? Meredith discounted the idea when she recalled thinking that he looked an active sort of man. Her impression of him was that he was a man who would have no time to waste on inconsequentials. Which made it certain that he would not have gone to the trouble of finding out her telephone number if all he wanted to do was to play some game. Surely, if her impression of him was correct, it must mean that, since he had gone to the trouble of finding her phone number, he must be interested in her—and not...

Her heartbeat went into overdrive again. Was Ryan Carlisle interested in her? It seemed so. As she sifted through everything it came to her that, since her phone number was listed under the name of Simmons, and not Maybry—the name he must have remembered from seeing her security name-tag yesterday—he must have asked more than one question about her. For a start, he would have had to make an enquiry of the chief window-dresser. Then, having got the information that she worked for an agency, he would have somehow had to inveigle her phone number from them. And that was not all. Since her name-tag had given only her initial 'M', and he had called her 'Meredith', he must have found out her first name; and not only that, but somehow, since he had said, 'I'll call for you', he had found out where she lived!

For the following ten minutes she didn't know whether to believe that Ryan Carlisle really did know where she lived, or was just having her on. When at the end of those ten minutes the front door bell sounded, she could have cried with relief. Not wanting her great-aunt to disturb herself to answer the door—and it was a certainty that Uncle Porter would not move to answer it—Meredith, with butterflies fluttering madly in her insides, hurriedly left her room.

Ryan Carlisle, when she pulled back the door, was every bit as tall as she remembered him, and every bit as appealing. He had a strong face. His firm chin, his firm if well-shaped mouth, his straight, aristocratic nose and high, intelligent forehead all spoke of a man who knew where he was going, and, since she guessed that he was the owner of Carlisle Electronics, she guessed too that he had already got there.

'H-hello,' she greeted him on a husky note, her blue eyes meeting grey eyes that seemed to have taken in her firm chin, her shapely mouth, dainty nose and smooth forehead in return. 'Will you come in for a moment and meet my family?' she asked him politely, knowing full well that Uncle Porter would chase after her, clutching at his heart, if she dared to leave the house without first introducing her escort for the evening.

Great-Aunt Evelyn was sweetness itself when Meredith introduced Ryan. Meredith wished she could have said the same of her great-uncle.

'What time are you bringing her back?' he demanded to know of Ryan.

'What time would you like to come home, Meredith?'
Ryan turned to her to enquire, enchanting her further
by not turning a hair at her great-uncle's rudeness.

'Any time after dinner,' she said as easily as she could,
bearing in mind that she felt embarrassed to death and
for once exasperated with her demanding relative, feeling
that she could just as easily at that moment have told
her uncle that she was never coming home again.

The mood passed the instant she and Ryan were
outside, but once he had settled her inside his sleek car
which simply purred away from the kerb it became clear
to her that Ryan Carlisle missed nothing.

'Have you lived with your great-aunt and uncle for
very long?' he enquired.

'Since I was five,' she told him openly, having quickly
discovered that it was no figment of her imagination that
she truly had fallen in love with him at first sight, and
loving every moment of this, her most unexpected time
with him. 'My parents were killed in an accident when
I was five,' she explained, and, beginning to feel that
she was being a chatterbox but knowing that nerves had
something to do with it, for she was most reserved as a
rule, she told him, 'My grandfather was alive then, and
Grandfather had a strong sense of duty. So...' She paused
to take a gulp of breath. Although she really believed
she must be boring him out of his skull, she discovered
that she could not stop talking. 'So, naturally, it was
unthinkable that I should go to live with anyone but
them. Not,' she added, 'that there was anyone else to
go to.' Determinedly, she closed her mouth and bit down
on any more words which would have bubbled to the
surface.

To her relief, though, Ryan did not appear to think
her garrulous tongue out of the ordinary, but com-

mented, 'It seems you've inherited your grandfather's strong sense of duty.'

'Oh,' she said, and, not sure what he meant by that statement, she asked, 'Why do you say that?'

'I rather gained the impression that you'd as soon not return to your home tonight,' he replied.

About to quickly tell him that her great-aunt was a dear, and that her great-uncle really was not as bad as all that, Meredith suddenly had the most ghastly feeling that Ryan Carlisle thought her much more modern-minded than her old-fashioned upbringing allowed her to be. Suddenly, she had the most awful feeling that he thought she was in the habit of staying out all night with whoever her dinner companion was—and that he was sounding her out on that score!

She felt no end disappointed in him, though she guessed that he had not lived to be in his mid-thirties without a little experience of some of his dinner companions returning to his place for a nightcap. But, since it had been she who had tried to engage him in conversation to start with and who might thereby have given him the wrong impression of her—albeit that her remarks to him had been totally innocent—she nevertheless thought she should get it straight, right here and now, that she was not the 'sleeping-around' type.

'Oh, I always go home every night,' she told him, and for good measure, she added, 'without fail.' And then, having got that message across, she found she was babbling again, as she went on to qualify, 'That is, except when I went to stay with my very good friend Tessa Wallace in Little Haversham...'

By the time Ryan Carlisle was pulling up outside a smart-looking hotel, Meredith had told him all about

her artist friend in Derbyshire and about the sadness of
her losing her much-loved Duncan.

As Ryan escorted her into the restaurant of the hotel
and the head waiter, clearly valuing him as a favoured
customer, led them to a well-positioned table, Meredith
was thinking in terms of not opening her mouth again
for the rest of the evening. Nerves, pure and simple, were
responsible for her having suddenly become this prat-
tling female, and she hated the fact that Ryan was not
seeing her at her best.

For, even if she didn't know what her best was, she
wanted him to see her in a good light so that, if the gods
were really, really kind to her, he might ask her for another date.

Aware that she was being greedy in the one respect of
wanting to know more and more of him, Meredith found
that she had hardly any appetite for food. Though, when
Ryan looked at her after she had spent long enough
studying the menu, she decided that, since she had accepted an invitation to dine, it would be the height of
bad manners to say she felt she could not eat a scrap.

'I'll have the Stroganoff, I think,' she told him, and
found she was going off again when she added, 'I made
it once at home, but Uncle Porter said he didn't want
any more of "that foreign muck", so I haven't eaten
any since.' Firmly then she closed her mouth. But to her
relief, not to say joy, Ryan smiled at her as though her
related anecdote about her grouchy uncle had amused
him.

From then on, Meredith began to relax. She rather
guessed that Ryan's manner had a lot to do with that.
For he had a good line in funny anecdotes too, and as
the meal progressed she fell more and more under his
spell. She also became more and more relaxed, so that

the next time she became talkative it seemed to her to be not babbling this time, but more two adults having a conversation—even if the conversation they were having centred on the shares which her father had left her.

How they had got on to the subject of her worthless shares, she could never afterwards remember. Although, since she had died a thousand deaths each time she recalled the way she had blurted out to Ryan in the lift yesterday, 'I have interests in the electrical field too!', she was fairly certain that she had not been the one to bring the subject up. But such was Ryan's charm that she felt no embarrassment when she told him that evening, 'Of course, the shares weren't as worthless then as they are now. But then, the shares were never that important. It was the chance to get back at my grandfather that mattered.'

'Your father purchased them to spite your grandfather?' Ryan queried, keeping up with her very well, she realised, since she was not explaining this too brilliantly.

'Sort of,' she said, and could see nothing for it but to go back to the beginning. 'I don't think my grandfather ever wanted my mother to marry and thereby get away from his domination. Although, if he couldn't prevent her from marrying when she reached twenty-one, he was determined that she was certainly not going to marry any penniless office worker.'

'But she did?'

Meredith nodded, and quietly she told him all that over the years her great-aunt Evelyn had confided. 'Apparently my parents very nearly didn't get married at all because of the hell my grandfather gave them over my father's lack of finances.'

'Obviously they did marry, though,' Ryan smiled encouragingly.

Meredith smiled back. 'They did,' she said. 'But my father never forgave Grandfather that, through him, he so nearly lost the woman he loved. According to Great-Aunt Evelyn, the two were for ever afterwards at loggerheads.'

'You sound as though you're not totally convinced of that,' Ryan commented.

'Oh, I am,' she assured him quickly. 'But in any case, there's written proof in the way my father left his will.' For once she could see that Ryan was not keeping up with her, and, feeling comfortable with him, she went on to explain fully. 'It took my father some years to get on his feet financially, but by the time I had arrived he had his own department and was well able to keep a wife and family. He then began investing heavily in shares— the Burgess ones,' she smiled, and resumed, 'Aunt Evelyn believes that it was purely to infuriate her brother Ogden that my father took great pleasure in showing him the will he made on my fifth birthday. In his will, I was to inherit the shares when I was twenty-five but, should I marry before my twenty-fifth birthday, on the day I married the shares were to go to my husband. It was my father's way of telling Grandfather that he was determined I wouldn't suffer should Grandfather become my guardian and frown on any penniless suitor who came calling.'

'This way, your father would have seen to it that on your wedding day your husband became a wealthy man.' Ryan this time caught on straight away.

'That's right,' Meredith beamed at him. 'Of course, my father never dreamed that I'd be orphaned only a few months later. Though he'd had the tremendous satisfaction of infuriating my grandfather over the way he'd left his shares...' Her smile had gone when, quietly, she told Ryan, 'My father never knew that his hated father-in-law had the last laugh when the value of those shares started to decline until they became absolutely worthless.'

Just then the attentive waiter came again to their table to see if they required more coffee, and with a start of surprise Meredith saw that she had disposed of one decent-sized cupful without having the smallest memory of having done so.

'Yes, please,' she told the waiter, not because she wanted more coffee, but because she never wanted this evening to end, and she knew that once they left the restaurant Ryan would take her home and she would never see him again.

It delighted her when he too said he would have another cup, just as though he too did not want the evening to end. And her heart just flipped when, suddenly, she caught him looking at her hard and long. He smiled, though, when he saw himself observed, and a little while afterwards he settled the bill and they left the restaurant.

They were almost at her door and Meredith was aching for some way to extend the evening. But there was no way, and all too soon Ryan was escorting her from his car and up to her front door.

Almost then she asked him in for a cup of coffee, only to realise that she had missed out on the chance of that sounding like a natural invitation since, through her greed in wanting more time with him back at the restaurant, they were already swimming in coffee.

'Thank you for a very nice evening,' she told him politely as he handed her key back after he had unlocked the front door.

'Thank you, Meredith,' he answered smoothly, and although she wanted with all she had to stay talking to him, she somehow found the will to do just the opposite.

'Goodnight,' she said, and swiftly she put herself to the other side of the door.

In bed that night she hit the highest peak of her existence as she recalled that once or twice Ryan had seemed amused at a reference she made here and there—while at other memories she hit the darkest trough. Oh, my hat, she thought, I must have bored him silly with my prattle about my father's will!

She was still cringing over that when she began to feel uplifted, for there had been no need for her to feel at all disappointed in Ryan for having ideas of taking her to his bed. Moments later, though, she was accepting that what did disappoint her was that he had not even so much as tried to kiss her.

By the following morning, Meredith was keeping very much to herself her disappointment that Ryan Carlisle had not only shown no inclination to kiss her, but no desire either to want to take her out again—or even so much as hint at a second date.

'Did you have a nice time, dear?' her great-aunt asked at breakfast.

'Very nice,' Meredith replied, and she smiled, and Great-Uncle Porter grunted. Somehow, though, the fact that her uncle had chosen this morning to throw a fit of the 'moodies' barely impinged on her consciousness.

By Monday Meredith just knew that she was never going to hear from Ryan Carlisle. Which made her very surprised when that evening, as she was on the way to the dining-room for her evening meal, she darted into the sitting-room to answer the phone en route and heard Ryan on the line.

Her surprise was total, and was perhaps the reason for her quite spontaneous exclamation of, 'I didn't expect to hear from you again!'

'It's your shares I'm after,' he teased, and, hearing a smile in his voice, Meredith loved him all the more that he should make the way she had bored him over those shares seem to be their own private joke. 'I know I've left it late, but I'm still at the office. Can you have dinner with me in an hour?'

Swiftly Meredith thought of both her aunt and uncle already seated round the dinner-table, just waiting for her to join them before they began their meal. Against a mental picture of Uncle Porter's dark displeasure if she did not join them, though, she put her feeling that Ryan Carlisle was not a man who asked again, once refused.

'Yes,' she said, and wasted no time once he had put his phone down before racing to the dining-room to tell her relatives to start without her.

Then, having left Aunt Evelyn dealing with Uncle Porter's cross, 'Well, I call that the giddy limit!' she hurried back upstairs to view her wardrobe with renewed displeasure, knowing that she just could not wear the black again.

There were a few minutes to go before Ryan called for her when, having opted for a mid-calf skirt of gold with a matching waistcoat and cream silk blouse, Meredith realised that her throat just called out for a fine gold chain to complete the outfit.

Since Uncle Porter insisted that her jewel case—not that she had too much in it—should be covered with

clothing and left to repose in the bottom drawer of her
chest of drawers, it took only a moment for her to stoop
to retrieve it. As she did so, however, her eyes lighted
on the buff-coloured folder which had lain there for some
while now. On impulse Meredith took the folder with
its contents from its usual home.

When a minute later the front door bell sounded, the
fine gold chain was secured around her throat and, as
she went quickly to leave her room, she took with her
the folder which she had taken out on impulse.

'I shan't be late back,' she called to her relatives, who
were now in the sitting-room. And, since they had already
met her escort, she saw no reason to ask Ryan in—he
must be starving anyway—and went sailing on to meet
him. 'I thought you might like to see my share certificates,' she told him with a grin, when his glance encom-
passed the folder she had in her hands—and so began
the second most wonderful evening of her life.

She was less garrulous on that dinner-date than she
had been on the previous one, but she had still done her
fair portion of talking when, with the time nearing midnight, Ryan took her home.

'Thank you,' she said as he drew the car up outside
her home and cut the engine.

'Thank you, Meredith,' he said, and she knew that in
the darkness he was smiling.

When Ryan helped her from his car and walked with
her to her front door, her heart was going like a trip
hammer. He had sounded as though he had enjoyed the
evening too—would he ask her out again?

He did not ask her out again, but what he did do was
to take her by the arms, and gently kiss her.

She sighed blissfully as he broke his brief kiss and let
go of her. Her sigh, though, seemed to halt him, and

his voice sounded just a trifle curt when he demanded, 'Hell's bells, was that your first kiss?'

Meredith rapidly came to, to realise that somehow or other through the evening Ryan must have picked up a hint that she did not have very much experience. Her naïve response to his kiss just now must have shown that too, she guessed. 'Of course it wasn't,' she told him, however, not wanting her marvellous evening with him to end on a sour note. 'Why, Aldo and I . . .'

'Spare me the details,' Ryan cut her off, and, taking her key from her, he unlocked the front door and pushed it wide. 'Goodnight,' he said, and strode back to his car.

Meredith sighed again as she climbed the stairs to bed. This time, though, her sigh was anything but blissful. Her trouble was, she realised, that she had barely any experience of men, and, living with her relatives the way she did, with Uncle Porter playing up on the few occasions she did go out, she did not see how she was going to gain any experience. She had just intimated to Ryan that she had experienced some degree of lovemaking with Aldo. But all she had received from Aldo, Tessa's older brother by four years, was an experimental kiss which she had not liked very much at all.

Wishing that she had been out with dozens of men, and that she was smart and sophisticated, Meredith climbed into bed, blushing under the bedclothes when she realised just how gauche she must seem to Ryan. So much for her enthusiasm in greeting him with, 'I thought you might like to see my share certificates'—he had not even glanced at them!

Realising that she had been so taken with her marvellous evening that she had forgotten to retrieve her buff folder from Ryan's car, but had left it here, Meredith

silently groaned as she also remembered that a copy of
her father's will lay inside it too.

'Oh, grief!' she murmured in anguish, and, remembering how she must have bored the socks off Ryan on
Saturday when she had spoken in detail of her father,
her grandfather and that wretched will, she hoped with
all she had that the folder containing both share certificates and the will had somehow managed to slide under
the luxurious carpet in Ryan's car—well out of sight.

She got up the next morning knowing that if she was
ever lucky enough to see Ryan again—though she was
firmly of the opinion that two dates with her had been
sufficient for him and that there would not be a third—
then never ever was she going to mention again the word
shares, nor the word will.

Against all her expectations, though, she did see Ryan
again. For he rang her that same afternoon, and, to her
great joy, asked her to dine with him that evening.

'I'd like that,' she told him, the understatement of the
year, she thought, and put down the phone to have to
face her demanding uncle.

'You're not going out with that man again tonight,
are you?' he questioned her grumpily, and when she said
that she was, he was at his most miserable, and contrary
with it.

'Ignore him—he's got a touch of the Ogdens,' her aunt
advised.

But a fractious Uncle Porter was difficult to ignore
and, run ragged by an over-demanding uncle, Meredith
was not skilled in hiding her feelings when Ryan arrived.

'What sort of a day have you had?' he asked percep-
tively once they were seated in his car.

'Oh, to get away from it all!' she replied, and, having
meant her words to come out jokily, she was appalled

when it sounded as though she had just about had enough of her elderly relatives. Quickly she put a smile into her voice, and brightly bounced a cheerful question back at him. 'What sort of day have *you* had?' she asked.

That dinner followed the same pattern as her dinner date with him last night. Ryan was a witty conversationalist and countless were the times he made her laugh. In no time at all, she had forgotten every bit about how grouchy her great-uncle had been.

When the time came for Ryan to drive her home, Meredith was feeling so much at ease with him that, not wanting the evening ever to end, she asked him if he would care to come in for a coffee.

'Yes, I should,' he replied without hesitation, but, to her everlasting delight, he seemed to be more interested in her when he followed her into the kitchen. And no sooner had she picked up the coffee jar than he took it out of her hand and placed it down on a working surface. 'What a lovely creature you are,' he murmured, and, while her heart started to thunder so loudly that she was sure that he must hear it, he reached for her and gathered her into his arms.

His first kiss on her mouth was warm and gentle. But, not wanting the evening to end on the same curt note as the previous evening, so that he should know that she was not some naïve miss, Meredith put her arms around him and clung to him.

His reaction, though, stunned her and made her aware that neither she nor her old-fashioned upbringing were yet ready for this. For his kiss changed to become ardent, and as he pulled her body close up to his, while part of her wanted to respond madly and she leant against him, one of his hands caressed from her back and came to cup her left breast in a tender hold.

With her body beginning to tingle with an emotion entirely new to her, Meredith gasped and pulled back out of his embrace, some part of her brain registering that her great-uncle would have a heart attack which would prove fatal if he chanced this moment to come down the stairs.

'I...' she gasped, wanting most urgently to be back in Ryan's arms, while at the same time needing time to adjust to this intimate side of loving. 'I...' she repeated, wanting quite desperately to say something that would nullify any curt word of parting he had for her.

But, to her gratitude, when she looked at Ryan's expression it was to observe that he did not appear to be curt or angry at all, but more good-humoured than anything.

Proof that he had indeed stayed good-humoured was to be seen in the way he touched a finger under her chin and, referring to what she had begun to say last night drawled softly, 'Whatever went on between "Aldo" and you, my dear, it didn't go beyond a few kisses.' And while Meredith had started to tingle anew, Ryan shattered her completely when, swamping her with his charm, he said, 'It seems to me, little virgin, that since I'm not to be allowed my "wicked way" without marriage, you'd better marry me without delay.'

'You—want—t-to marry me!' Meredith choked incredulously.

'Without delay,' Ryan repeated, his eyes watchful on hers.

'Oh, Ryan!' she cried, and just had to ask, 'You love me?'

His answer was to take her into his arms and gently kiss her. And she had all the proof she wanted that he loved her, for when a man like Ryan said 'without delay' he meant just that. Already he was sweeping her off her feet by telling her that with a special licence they could be married by the weekend.

Thrilled in a way she had never in her twenty-two years experienced, Meredith was ready to agree to anything he said. Years of living with her great-aunt and great-uncle, though, were not so easily discarded.

'I can't be ready by then!' she just had to tell him, and she itemised, 'I have to tell my aunt and uncle, then I'll have to fill up the freezer and see to it that they...'

'So, OK, I'll give you two extra days,' he conceded, and thrilled her yet again when he said firmly, 'But I insist, Meredith, that you don't make me wait longer than next Monday.'

The sound of the front door opening brought Meredith out of her reverie. For here it was, Monday, and here she was in her going-away outfit, and she should have gone downstairs ages ago.

With her heart overflowing with happiness, she hurriedly left her seat to go swiftly from her bedroom for the last time. Her attack of nerves was over, and more than anything she wanted to be with Ryan, her husband.

Already as she sped silently along the landing she could hear his voice as he saw his friend and best man, Monte Montgomery, on his way. She had known that Monte Montgomery had an appointment later, and it vexed her that she had stayed in her room so long when she should have been by Ryan's side to say goodbye to their guest.

A moment of shyness took her, however, and when she was about to round the landing and go down the stairs she paused. And that was when Monte Montgomery's voice took over from Ryan's and floated up the stairs. And that was when her world came crashing down about her.

For, 'My stars, Ryan, you must be the jammiest devil I know,' she clearly heard his friend say jovially. 'Not only do you get those shares you've wanted for so long—but the woman you have to take with them just happens to be beautiful!'

Stopped dead in her tracks when she would have gone on, Meredith was bewildered by what Monte Montgomery was saying. But when it quickly dawned on her that he was saying that Ryan had married her not because he loved her but because of the shares, she stayed where she was, sure that Ryan would put his friend right in no uncertain terms.

But her husband of a few hours did not put his friend right. To the contrary, Meredith, in utter disbelief, actually heard Ryan—*agreeing* with him!

'It takes the edge off having to marry at all that my bride just happens to be beautiful,' she heard him admit, and, as the colour started to drain from her face, she heard him add, 'But to own those shares I'd have married her had she looked like the rear end of a horse.' Meredith was clutching on to the stair-rail as though her life depended upon it when he tacked on cheerfully, 'It's a bonus, of course, that she's a biddable little thing, and...'

At that point, Meredith could not bear to hear any more. With pain tearing away at her insides, she returned to the bedroom as noiselessly as she had come from it. The small wedding party was waiting for her to join them downstairs, but, with her heart starting to break, she needed to think.

CHAPTER TWO

WITH her world falling apart around her, Meredith was so distraught by what she had just heard that, having fled to her bedroom, needing to think, she discovered that any chance of clear thinking was impossible. The words '... to own those shares, I'd have married her had she looked like the rear end of a horse' were spinning around in her head, and all she knew for sure was that Ryan Carlisle had not married her because he loved her, but because to marry her was the only way in which he could get his hands on her shares. Why he should want her worthless shares was not important to her just then. All that was important was that Ryan, her husband, the man she loved so very much, did not love her.

Some noise from downstairs broke into her unhappiness and panicked her into going to the door of her room. Crazily the notion passed through her mind that, if she did not soon show herself downstairs, Ryan might come looking for her. Why, in the light of what she had just learned, she should think he would do that, she was unsure, but she was not yet ready to face him on a one-to-one level, and so quickly she left her room.

She was at the door of the sitting-room when she realised that she did not want to see anyone else either. But Mrs Key, who was there that day partly as a guest and partly to dispense food and drink, suddenly came from the direction of the kitchen.

'You look almost as lovely in your going-away suit as you did in your wedding dress,' their daily help crooned when Meredith, spotting the tray of tea in her hands, opened the sitting-room door for her.

Somehow, because it was expected of her, Meredith managed to pin a smile on her face as she stood back to allow the tea-carrying Mrs Key to go into the room first. Somehow, too, she managed to hold that smile in place as her glance flicked past Ryan, who was in conversation with their elderly next-door neighbour, Mrs Peplow, and went to where her great-aunt Evelyn appeared to be having a few cross words with her brother Porter.

Uncle Porter's colour was much too high, Meredith thought, though whether from too much champagne or too much excitement, she could not tell. In her view, though, he'd had enough excitement for one day. She would do him no good at all, she realised, if she suddenly gave way to the hurt that was screaming away inside her and created a scene.

'Shall we go, my dear?' Ryan's coming silently to her side and asking the cool, relaxed question brought Meredith down from a hysterical pitch. She had never created a scene in her life, for goodness' sake, so she wasn't likely to start now—and certainly not in front of her aged relatives!

Which fact, although she had been undecided what she should do, or where she should go, finally brought her the answer. For the sake of her great-aunt's peace of mind, and out of respect for her great-uncle's dodgy heart, she would go with her husband. What happened after that she had not quite decided.

'I'll just say my goodbyes,' she told Ryan quietly, and went first to have a word with Mrs Key, having previously arranged with that good lady that she would ring her at her new home if she was at all worried about either of her relatives. Next, and because she had known Mrs Peplow nearly all her life, she went and kissed her goodbye, and then she went and said goodbye to her aunt and uncle.

'I suppose we're never going to see you now that you're married,' her uncle said grumpily, the champagne he had consumed not improving his temper.

'Don't start, Porter!' his sister warned him, and motioned to Meredith to go now, since it did not look as though his manner was going to get any better.

'I'll—be in touch,' Meredith told her aunt huskily, giving her a swift hug. And in the early evening of what was turning out to be the worst day of her life, she went quickly out to where Ryan's car was standing at the kerb.

There had been a brief let-up in the hurt and pain screaming away at her as she had said her goodbyes. But as Ryan got into the car beside her and began to drive off, the pain and hurt he had caused her returned in full force.

'You're very quiet,' he said when they had been driving for some minutes and she had volunteered not a word.

Uncertain if he was saying that it made a pleasant change to have her quiet after the chatterbox she had occasionally been prone to being, Meredith swallowed down more hurt. 'It's been a busy day,' she told him evenly.

Busy was not the word for it, she thought as she recalled how prior to that day she had raced around like a mad thing because she had thought Ryan impatient to marry her. Oh, he'd been impatient to marry her, true enough, but not because he loved her. Oh, what a fool she had been!

All the while she had dashed around—shopping for the home, shopping for herself, cooking for the freezer—

she had believed he loved her. Willingly, wanting to marry him as much as she had thought he wanted to marry her, she had done the hundred and one things that had to be done in order to be ready for today. In the belief that he loved her, and with no time to spare in which to go to see the inside of his apartment—her new home—she had happily packed a suitcase of her favourite clothes. And Ryan, with every appearance of looking forward to this day as much as she, had taken the case to his apartment for her.

But he *had* been looking forward to this day, she suddenly realised. Not because he was impatient for her, but because he was impatient to get his hands on her shares.

He had wanted her shares so badly that he had been prepared to marry her had she looked like the rear end of a horse, she recalled painfully. He had not wanted to marry at all, though, really—she did not have to look past his 'It takes the edge off having to marry at all that my bride just happens to be beautiful' to know that.

Suddenly then, though, Meredith was recalling what else Ryan had said, and as she remembered how cheerfully he had said, 'It's a bonus, of course, that she's a biddable little thing,' she started to get angry. And, having left the restraints of her upbringing, she began to feel less and less *biddable* the nearer she got to her new home.

She welcomed the feeling of anger. The pain was still there, but to feel angry too was a great help. She had grown up knowing that she did not possess a temper but, dammit, there were limits!

The locale where Ryan had his apartment was salubrious-looking, and expensive. As they went in he introduced Preston, the smartly uniformed hall security man, and then, having referred to her as 'my wife', he was escorting her over to the lift.

But Meredith did not feel the thrill which she would have felt an hour earlier to be spoken of as 'my wife'. She did not feel like a wife, and as they stepped out of the lift and Ryan unlocked the door of his apartment, and her anger went up another notch, she decided that she was not going to be a wife to him.

She knew that for certain when, having closed the door to the outside world, and just as though he believed it was expected of him, her new husband made as though to take her in his arms.

With her expression stony, Meredith evaded him. To show how concerned he was *not* by her actions, she saw him shrug as his arms fell back to his sides. Nor did he make any attempt to take hold of her again, but he allowed her to cross over the hall and walk down the three thickly carpeted steps into his large, thickly carpeted and luxurious sitting-room.

And it was there, in the middle of his sitting-room, that nerves, anger, and hurt all fused into one within her. Without a glimmer of a smile on her face, Meredith turned, and, while she was quite well aware that he had no idea she had overheard him in conversation with Monte Montgomery, she asked shortly, 'Why did you marry me?'

She saw the alert look in his eyes, but he was cool, and appeared still in a fine good humour, drawling, 'It seemed a good idea at the time.'

But Meredith could see nothing to be good-humoured about, and silently she stared at him with her brilliantly blue eyes. To his credit, though, Ryan was not a man who would look away from trouble. And after waiting a minute longer for her to follow up if she was going to, he took the initiative from her.

'I refuse to begin our marriage with you going into a fit of sulks over some imagined slight,' he told her bluntly, good humour nowhere to be seen.

'*Imagined* slight!' she exclaimed, part of her idiotic enough to want him good-humoured with her again, while the saner side of her was ready to be up in arms that he should dare to accuse her of having a fit of sulks.

'Something's been festering away in you ever since we left your aunt and uncle's home,' he went on brusquely, and while she was giving him ten out ten for perception, he was ordering, 'So out with it—let's have it all!'

Meredith had a brief struggle with the person inside her who wanted Ryan to stay in a good humour, and a short tussle with the one who was trying to stay in the well-mannered—and biddable—mould of her up-bringing. But the mould had already started to crack, and she was discovering in herself a pride which refused to allow her to stay quiet and pretend that nothing had happened.

'How about—and I quote,' she began coolly, ' "To own those shares, I'd have married her had she looked like the rear end of a horse"?'

She saw it register with him that she must have over-heard his conversation with Monte Montgomery. But not by so much as a flicker of an eyelid did Ryan look as though he felt he had said anything to be ashamed of. Indeed—and she was watching him intently—it seemed to Meredith that he thought she had a fine cheek in listening to his conversation anyway!

He wasted no time, however, in squashing completely any lingering hope she might have that she had got it all wrong and that there must be some simple explanation,

when, as bluntly as before, he told her quite openly, 'Of
course I married you for those shares—if that's why
you're sulking.' And, while she was taking that on the
chin, he went on, 'So all right, perhaps I should have
told you that your shares in Burgess Electrical, far from
being worthless, as you thought them, have shot up in
value in recent months, but...'

'My sh...the shares—they aren't worthless?' she
questioned, still not very interested in the shares, but not
wanting him to see how his unfeeling confirmation that
he had not married her for love was rocking her
foundations.

'Not now,' he told her, and, openly still, he went on,
'Not now half the electronic firms in the business, mine
included, are waiting their chance to take Burgess
Electrical over.'

'Firms—your firm—want to take them over?' she
queried in surprise. She had never had a head for
business, but even with her limited comprehension of
what went on in big business, it did not seem to her to
be a very good investment. 'Burgess Electrical have been
ailing for years and years—to the point of extinction not
too many years ago,' she told Ryan, though she now
realised he probably already knew that anyway. 'So
wh...?'

'So why want to take them over?' he finished for her,
and, again openly, he told her, 'On account of the most
minute piece of antiquated equipment which they manu
facture. A piece of equipment which was dismissed as
obsolete, but which, it's now been discovered, can cut
production costs by huge amounts for whoever can get
hold of it. Unfortunately, Burgess Electrical hold the
patent, and are unwilling to sell it.'

'Which means that you, along with everyone else,' Meredith worked it out, 'are buying up Burgess Electrical shares as fast as you can.'

'Past tense,' Ryan grunted. Since she had been bright enough to stay with him this far, he went on, 'Everyone's already bought—there just aren't any more available. That is there weren't, until . . .'

He did not have to continue, for not only was Meredith keeping up with him, she had gone streaming on to work more out for herself. 'My godfathers!' she exclaimed. 'You must have thought you'd hit the jackpot that day in that lift when I told you that my father had left me thousands and thousands of Burgess Electrical shares!'

'I couldn't believe what I was hearing,' he admitted, and further owned, 'Nor could I believe my eyes when a look at the share certificates showed that your father was obsessed with buying more and yet more of them.'

'Nor could you believe your eyes, I suspect,' Meredith said acidly, 'when a sight of my father's will confirmed what I'd already told you—that those shares became the property of my husband should I marry before I reached my twenty-fifth birthday.'

'What are you complaining of?' Ryan queried, giving her a sharp look on hearing acid in her tones for the first time. 'I married you, didn't I—which was what you wanted?' And while Meredith immediately lost her acid feelings and was instead mortally wounded that he should so uncaringly refer to the love she bore him, he went on to startle her when he rapped, 'Be honest, Meredith. You couldn't wait to leave home. All you needed was a good excuse—and I provided it.'

For ageless seconds she just stared at him. She had received shock upon shock since marrying him, but as her wounded heart bled a little more, so her intelligent brain quickly grasped what he had said and she grabbed at the chance he had given her to keep her pride intact. By the sound of it, Ryan had no idea how very much she loved him. As far as he was concerned, she began to see, her eager response to his few kisses, and her eagerness to rush around doing all she had rushed around to do, including giving him a packed suitcase, all stemmed from her impatience to get away from her aunt and uncle!

'You're right, Ryan, of course,' she got herself sufficiently together to drawl, and, having remembered that she had a suitcase here somewhere, with some vague notion of collecting it and getting out of there, she asked, 'Can you tell me where you put the suitcase I gave you?'

'It's in a spare bedroom,' he replied, and unwittingly gave her a moment or two to get over yet more hurt. Quite clearly, she realised as he led the way back up the three steps and turned right along the hall to where the bedrooms were, he had never meant them to have a proper marriage anyway.

Suddenly, though, as she followed him to one of the spare bedrooms, Meredith realised the impossibility of returning to her old home. Oh, lord, she thought in anguish: apart from Aunt Evelyn's having a thing about what the neighbours would say, her aunt was of the school which believed that a woman, once married, stayed married, and remained with her husband no matter what.

The spare bedroom which Ryan took her to was completely furnished, and, glancing at the bed, Meredith felt all at once exhausted and as if she could sleep for a week. It was then that she saw she needed some time to make some sort of plans. It was then also that she saw that it was a bit late to think of checking into a hotel while she considered what to do.

'Is it all right with you if I make use of this room for...'

'Suit yourself,' Ryan cut her off, and sounded so uncaring that she knew she had been right when she had thought it had never been in his head for them to have a proper marriage. Though she was to wonder if she had got that quite right when, his good humour quite obviously returned, he murmured, 'It might have been interesting to teach you a few things, but you're your own person now. It's for you to decide what you want...'

'I can do without the lecture,' she told him shortly, and when he went from the room without another word she went over to her suitcase which was by the window and bent down to unlatch it.

She twisted round, though, and straightened up when, carrying bedlinen and towels, the man she had married came back into the room. 'That should cover the sleeping arrangements,' he said, placing his cargo down on the bed. 'There's a bathroom through there,' he added, pointing to another door in the room. Meredith suffered a weak moment and realised that, had he been—coaxing—and not matter-of-fact as he was, she might, even knowing what she did, have been persuaded to 'let him teach her a few things'. But even as she realised that, he was saying easily, 'I'll leave you to it. That is, unless you want anything to eat or...'

'I want nothing, thank you,' Meredith told him firmly, and while she had the strength she turned her back on him and knelt once more to her suitcase. There followed a taut moment of silence, then, quietly, the door was closed. Swiftly she jerked around to check, but she was alone.

Ashamed of her wanton feelings of a moment ago, she went and switched on the small bedside light, and then switched off the centre light in the room. Then she moved the linen Ryan had brought in from the bed and, kicking off her shoes, lay down on the coverlet. Once or twice just recently she had thought she had been a bit of an idiot, but as the seconds and then the minutes ticked by, and then the hours started to pass, she recognised that she had been more than plain idiotic.

No wonder she had experienced the occasional moment of disquiet when thinking of the love she'd believed Ryan had for her! Some sixth sense must have been at work trying to tell her she had got it all wrong. Not that she would have listened anyway, she realised. She had wanted to believe he loved her, and she would not have heeded any logical voice that insisted on asking why a sophisticated man like him should be interested in unsophisticated her.

Oh, Meredith Maybry—Meredith Carlisle, she corrected herself—however could you have been such a fool as to allow yourself to believe, just because you had fallen in love with him at first sight, that he had done the same?

Life was just not like that, she realised, and suddenly she found she was in the painful process of growing up overnight. A stray tear or two could not be held back as she now accepted Ryan's words for the truth they had been when he said, 'It's your shares I'm after.' Oh, lord— had she been green!

And how very worldly he had been, she realised. She was dry-eyed when, as dawn approached, she began to break free of the placid mould she had been in all her life. The swine, she thought angrily: he had known what he was about the whole time!

Too angry suddenly to lie there any longer, Meredith got up from the bed and, sorting through her suitcase, extracted fresh underwear, trousers and a sweater, and took them with her to the adjoining bathroom. She grew more angry than ever with the man she had yesterday married as she quickly removed her going-away outfit and set about having a wash and changing her clothes.

Like a lamb to the slaughter, she had not only presented him with the proof he needed that she did have share certificates for thousands upon thousands of Burgess Electrical in her possession, but she had also given him free access to her father's will!

Why, she'd like to bet that both the will and the share certificates had been handed over to his lawyers the very next morning to see if there was any loophole that would see him married to her for nothing.

She drummed up more anger against him when, since she could not see him taking anything at face value, she thought it highly probable that he had again contacted the agency she had worked for, this time to check that she had not yet reached her twenty-fifth birthday.

When the small voice of fairness arrived to point out that Ryan had believed he was doing her something of a favour, in that by marrying her he had given her a chance to know something different in life from service to her aging relatives, Meredith deliberately turned her back on it. That altruistic he wasn't! If it hadn't been for those shares he would never have phoned asking her out to dinner in the first place. Ryan Carlisle had known exactly what he wanted, and had gone straight for it. He might be too busy to go away on honeymoon—not that he'd had any such intent—but he would not be too busy to have those shares transferred to his name, would he?

Daylight had filtered through the early April morning when a trouser- and sweater-clad Meredith returned to the bedroom. Packing the clothes she had just changed from into her case, she fastened the locks and hefted it up.

She opened the bedroom door, remembering the way she had left her family home out of concern for her great-uncle's dicky heart. She made her way to the main door, having no clear idea of where she was going, but knowing only that, while it was unthinkable that she return to her old home, for the moment anyway, it was equally unthinkable that she should stay on here—where, most obviously, she was not wanted.

Meredith had thought her feelings were frozen over as she put her suitcase down prior to unlatching the main door of the apartment. But when Ryan's voice abruptly addressed her, startling her into turning around, she knew from the sudden pounding of her heart that, though she had grown up rapidly in these last hours, she still loved him.

'Where in hell's name do you think you're going?' he barked, as on bare feet he strode along the hall from his bedroom towards her.

Meredith was more familiar with seeing Ryan clean-shaven and immaculately turned out, but as she noted the stubble on his chin and the way his hair was ruffled as though he had been fast asleep when some sound had disturbed him, he seemed more dear to her than ever. But her heart had led her astray before, and while it did the most peculiar things to her insides to see from the short robe he had thrown about him that he must have little else on, she hardened her heart. Even as it dawned on her that for him to ask where she was going must mean that he had been prepared to let her carry on living

there for a while, Meredith was denying every one of
her weaknesses.

Spurring on hate against him, for the first time in her
life she used sarcasm, as she told him loftily, 'I'll let you
have my forwarding address.'

She could see from the slight narrowing of his eyes
that he did not care very much for her manner, nor for
this hint that she had changed somewhat from the docile
female he thought her.

His voice had taken on a definite degree of coolness,
at any event, when, fixing his eyes firmly on the blue of
hers, he drawled, 'I take it that you're not returning
whence you came?'

He *is* a swine, she thought as, reading his comment
for the sarcastic offering it was, she started to grow angry.
For as she recalled their most recent conversation, it did
not take much for her to realise that his belief that she
would not return to her old home in a hurry stemmed
from his certainty that all she had wanted had been some
good excuse to escape from it in the first instance. Her
anger was doubly fired as she realised too that Ryan did
not care a snap of the fingers where she went. It did not
matter a jot to him what she did, now that he had got
control of those shares.

'You know quite well that I shan't be returning to my
family!' she told him sharply as her anger against him
began to peak. She was aware that her emotions were
getting out of control, but she held on tightly to the one
fact that Ryan believed she had married him to get away
from her family.

Unable to concentrate on more than her desire not to
give him any idea that to return to the safe, if dull, haven
of her old home had quite some appeal, Meredith found
that she could no longer keep her buffeted emotions

under control when Ryan, at his most arrogant, aloofly drawled, 'Then, my dear, I insist you allow me to provide for you.' It was not offensive enough that he should use the same endearment which had once thrilled her but which most clearly he did not mean, but Meredith's already weakening grip on her emotions was lost when, sarcastically, he added, 'What sort of a husband would I be if, having saved you from your...'

What adjective he would have chosen to denigrate her family, Meredith did not wait to find out. But, certain that he was about to say something of a derogatory nature about her great-aunt and great-uncle, she remembered how he had referred to her confidently as a 'biddable little thing' and suddenly she was inflamed. In a flash she had sent her right hand arcing through the air and had caught him the most perfect, and to her the most satisfying, blow to the side of his face.

Nor was she repentant. That blow, she realised, had been on its way for some hours and had little to do with any remarks he might choose to use on her family. With yet more satisfaction, she saw how totally astonished Ryan was at this change from biddable to passionate. His chin jutted an angry fraction when she refused to look in any way sorry for her action, but then Meredith, with veritable sparks flashing in her brilliant blue eyes, suddenly observed something very much akin to admiration come to the grey depths of his eyes.

A moment later she was doubting that he admired any part of her—she had been fooled before -oh, how she'd been fooled! Which was why she acted quickly, before her imagination should lead her on a false trail which would undermine this new person she had discovered in herself. 'You'll never know, *my dear*,' she told him, 'just how much I enjoyed doing that!' With that she had the door open and, picking up her case, she left her husband of less than twenty-four hours.

In the lift her head was too full of Ryan for her to think where she was going now. But, as she stepped from the lift and Preston, who had been on duty when she arrived, came over and took her case from her, she realised that she had better do some thinking, and fast.

Whether he had been on duty all the while or whether he had been off duty and had come on again, she had no idea. But all her fast thinking brought her nothing other than the knowledge that it was too early for her to check into any hotel. She was therefore grateful to him when, just as though it had occurred to him on seeing her with her case that she had been called urgently away, he suggested, 'A taxi to the station, is it, madam?'

'Yes, please,' she replied.

He was already at his switchboard and on to the taxi service when, 'Which railway station would you be requiring, Mrs Carlisle?' he asked.

Meredith told him the only one she had used in London. 'St Pancras,' she instructed him.

CHAPTER THREE

THE one good thing about railway stations, Meredith mused glumly as she sat pondering what best to do next, was that one could sit, seemingly staring into space, at any odd time of the day or night, and no one took a blind bit of notice. To add authenticity to her façade of being a traveller, she had her large suitcase beside her.

She realised that she must have been searching for some kind of anonymity when she had eagerly grabbed at Preston's suggestion that she might want a taxi to the station.

Feeling exhausted and used up, she tried to concentrate on what she should do—dwelling over the past was not going to be any help. Tiredly she went over the options she had open to her. She could return to her great-aunt and great-uncle, but abruptly she shied away from the idea of doing that. She felt as appalled at the prospect of having to tell them that her marriage was over as they would be to receive such news. Besides, with all her hopes and dreams suddenly turned into ashes, she felt much too hurt inside to withstand any lecture from her great-aunt on the fact that, no matter what, her place was with her husband and not with them.

Meredith guessed that her lack of sleep last night was not conducive to her feeling any great enthusiasm for lugging her suitcase with her while she looked round for a modestly priced hotel.

She glanced at her watch and saw that it was a quarter to eight. For no reason, some quirk in her memory department prodded to remind her that it had been on this very station eighteen months ago that she had caught the quarter to eight train to Derby.

Her thoughts strayed to her good friend Tessa and to how yesterday she had wanted her there at her wedding. But for everything having been arranged at such short notice, Meredith knew that she would have been there. Tessa, though, had put some considerable time and energy into getting the elderly in the village of Little Haversham interested in art, and had got an art class running, and yesterday was the culmination of a year's efforts when they were having an exhibition of work.

'Oh, Meredith,' she had wailed when Meredith had excitedly telephoned her to ask her to be there, 'I can't come!' She had then sought round for different ways of being in two places at once, and they had both ended up laughing, as Meredith had told her, 'I'll send you a piece of wedding cake.'

How long ago that telephone conversation now seemed, Meredith thought, her only piece of good fortune being that Tessa had not been able to attend her fiasco of a wedding. The way things had turned out, the fewer people who witnessed it, the better.

Suddenly then, through her fatigue, Meredith all at once began to see that maybe to have recalled catching the train to Derby had not been any stray quirk at all. It was then that she began to see that there might be another option open to her. Indeed, the more she thought about it, the more it seemed to be the obvious option. What she needed more than anything right now was to get away to somewhere where she could take a long and, if possible, unemotional view of what had happened.

She knew without question that Tessa would offer her a warm welcome, but she hesitated. She'd had every intention of visiting her old home once a week at least, although, in the belief that she would be living with Ryan in his apartment, she had given Mrs Key his phone number in case of an emergency. Mrs Key was not the type to panic, and both Great-Aunt Evelyn and Great-Uncle Porter had seemed all right—was it only yesterday? Meredith recalled how she had meant to telephone to check on her family during this week, but she could as easily do that from Tessa's, she considered.

Anyway, she realised as she suddenly made up her mind and went looking for a telephone, she rather thought that, since this was supposed to be her honeymoon, they would not expect to hear anything of her for at least a week.

'Meredith!' Tessa squealed when she answered her phone and heard her friend on the other end. 'What the heck are you doing ringing me?' she exclaimed. 'You're on your honeymoon!'

'Actually,' Meredith said chokily, holding back sudden and unexpected emotional tears, 'I'm not.'

'You didn't... Didn't you get married yesterday, after all?' Tessa rephrased her question.

'I—did,' Meredith told her. 'But I—it's a long story,' she added raggedly, and on a shaky breath she asked, 'Can I come and stay?'

Meredith knew Tessa for a true friend when, after the barest pause while she assimilated what she had said and that she had used the singular 'Can *I* come and stay' and not *'we'*, plus her ragged, shaky tone, she did not ask any questions.

'Of course,' she told Meredith. 'Come and stay as long as you like. If you can get to St Pancras in time, there's a train which Aldo sometimes catches which leaves at nine—I'll meet you,' she added.

Meredith spent the hour-and-a-half train journey getting herself more under control. But she faced the fact that she was not anywhere near as tough as she wanted to be when she saw her long-skirted, stick-thin friend, with her waist-length hair waving in the breeze, waiting for her at Derby station.

'I've still got the old banger,' Tessa said cheerfully, having given her a hug and against Meredith's protests grabbed her suitcase from her. 'As it's such a sunny day, I thought we'd drive with the top down.'

'You're getting more eccentric than ever,' Meredith told her, and went with her to where Tessa had parked her Morris Minor tourer.

'Do you want to talk about what happened?' Tessa asked gently when they were out in the country.

'There's not a great deal to tell,' Meredith replied, and realised only then that there wasn't. 'I fell in love at first sight with Ryan Carlisle, and didn't stop to think when he asked me to marry him within a week of our meeting——' she broke off as she remembered that he had not so much as asked her to marry him, but had told her that she had better marry him, without delay '—that he might not have fallen in love at first sight with me in return.'

'You've since learned that his feelings for you weren't so immediate?' Tessa queried.

'I've since learned that he has no feelings for me whatsoever,' Meredith told her bluntly.

'Oh, love,' said Tessa softly. 'Are you sure?'

'Oh, yes,' Meredith told her. 'I'm sure.' Somehow she managed to keep her voice even as she revealed how she had heard her husband of a few hours in conversation with his friend Monte Montgomery, and how Ryan had done nothing to conceal a thing when, later, he had taxed her with going into a fit of the sulks.

'What he needs is horse-whipping,' Tessa told her as she pulled the Morris up outside her cottage. 'And what you need,' she said as they went indoors, 'is a jolly good howl.'

'Will it do me any good?' Meredith asked hopefully.

'Not a scrap, I'm afraid,' Tessa told her.

The next two days passed in something of a haze for Meredith. She was aware of doing various chores, of mechanically eating and drinking, and of going for long walks with Tessa, but her head was still full of Ryan and her disaster of a marriage.

When she went to bed on Thursday night, though, she was so drained from lack of sleep that nature took over and she slept fairly well. She awoke on Friday morning with her usual first thought: how her marriage had not lasted twenty-four hours and how she would have given anything for it to be otherwise. But she was starting to emerge from her shock, both actual and delayed, and, having caught up on some of her missed sleep, she discovered that she had pride and sufficient backbone to cope.

'I'll make the toast,' she volunteered as she went down and joined Tessa in her kitchen.

'Sleep better?' asked Tessa, taking a long look at her.

'Much better,' Meredith answered, and found a smile as, aware that Tessa supplemented her part-time teaching income by painting and selling her watercolours, she told her, 'If you want to go out sketching today, I could clear up for you.'

'So you don't like my brand of cobwebs, huh?' Tessa laughed, having more important things on her mind than to consider getting the vacuum cleaner out more than

once every three months. 'I tell you what, though—I've
an idea that Aldo might turn up some time after he's
finished his stint at his advertising agency tonight—if
you're feeling really like working, you could muck out
the boxroom so I can put a camp bed in there for him
if he shows.'

'He can have my room,' Meredith promptly asserted.

'He can *not*!' Tessa told her firmly.

'But he's your brother, and . . .'

'And you're my friend,' Tessa butted in. 'Besides, you
were here first. And anyway, he may have resolved his
differences with Caroline, his live-in girlfriend, and might
not be giving Little Haversham a second's thought this
weekend.'

Meredith sincerely hoped for Aldo's sake that he was
having better luck in his love-life than she was having
in hers. She did not want him to be hurt. She had always
liked him and at one time she'd had a tiny crush on him.
She had been completely cured, though, the instant he
had kissed her that time. She did not know what she
had expected—perhaps bells to ring, or something like
that—but nothing in any way magical had happened,
except that, having wondered what it would be like if he
ever kissed her, she'd known then that she did not want
him to kiss her again, and known also that she was over
her crush.

As soon as Tessa had loaded up her car with her artist's equipment and had driven off, Meredith set to work
on the boxroom. She felt better for having something to
give her energies to, though she could not stop thoughts
of Ryan from attacking.

The boxroom was small, and did not take long to put
in apple-pie order. Finding homes for the clutter and
impedimenta took longer. But, after she had stacked

everything away neatly and tidily, it was still early when Meredith set about mucking out the rest of the rooms, with the exception of her friend's bedroom, which she considered private.

Discovering, however, that Tessa did not have a great deal in the way of cleaning materials, she decided to take a trip to the village's general store. While she was there, she would look for something tasty for dinner. Tessa had been a perfect angel ever since she had got here— to make dinner for her for a change would be the least she could do.

Taking her purse, Meredith was soon discovering that 'general store' did not begin to cover the emporium that served the village and anyone who happened to be passing through. Spotting one or two specialised items, she saw that the enterprising store owner had a range of goods to be purchased that was as wide as it was various.

Meredith had taken her self-service basket to the till, and the smart, businesslike woman was just reaching for the last of the articles from the basket when, with her mind on the Normandy chicken recipe they would have that evening, Meredith suddenly realised that she needed apple juice.

'Have you any apple juice?' she asked quickly, being unable to see any from where she was standing.

'Apple juice, Sidney!' the woman yelled, and from the sounds of flurried activity somewhere outside her vision, Meredith supposed that a carton of apple juice would soon be to hand. 'Are you journeying far?' the woman whom Meredith took to be the store owner asked, to pass the time while they waited.

'I'm staying with a friend in the village, actually,' Meredith smiled.

'Oh, you'll be Tessa Wallace's friend,' the store owner stated, and, while Meredith was still blinking as she wondered how the dickens she knew that, the woman was asking, 'Are you an artist too?'

Meredith shook her head, but even as she smiled as she realised that the village KGB didn't know everything, from the corner of her eye she spotted a part of a well-known financial paper peeping out from beneath some magazines on display. 'I'll take this too,' she said, pulling the paper out and, as a thin wiry man arrived with her apple juice, she thanked him for his trouble.

'That paper isn't today's—it's yesterday's,' the woman told her.

'I'll take it just the same,' Meredith smiled, and she left the store, thinking that there wouldn't be too much difference in the change in the price of Burgess Electrical shares from yesterday to today.

But from what Ryan had said, there must be a vast difference from the last time she had checked on them. Which, she realised, must be all of five years ago—if not longer.

While Grandfather had been alive they'd had a financial paper delivered every Saturday. But, since it had been only he who had read it, Great-Uncle Porter had cancelled it when his brother Ogden had died. The fact that Burgess Electrical shares were not quoted in the financial columns of the daily paper they took did not—since the shares had come to be virtually worthless—concern any of them.

When she got back to the cottage, though, Meredith knew a strange reluctance to check in the paper for the price of the Burgess shares. She knew quite well that she was using delaying tactics when first she set the kettle to boil, then put the cleaning materials ready to use later, and put the apple juice along with some chicken pieces she had bought in the fridge. Next she made herself a cup of coffee, and, the moment to be delayed no longer, she took up the paper and opened it out at the relevant page.

Some minutes later she was still reeling from the shock of seeing that the price of each share, multiplied by the many thousands she'd had in her possession, represented a small fortune!

By the time she had finished her coffee, though, Meredith was over her shock. She could not have laid claim to the shares for nearly another three years anyway. And, the way things seemed destined to be for her, she calculated that by the time she did reach the twenty-five years of age which her father had stipulated, the chances were that the shares would be worthless again anyway.

Not long afterwards she rinsed out her coffee-mug, and returned to her cleaning. She could not but be struck by the irony of the way things had turned out, though. For, while in making the will he had wanted purely to score a few points of her grandfather, in not changing it before he had died, her father had most definitely left things the last way in which he must have wanted them. Because of the hurt both he and her mother had suffered at the hands of her grandfather, her father, Meredith was sure, had intended that she should never suffer such hurt too. Although he had anticipated that the shares would increase in value, what he had not thought of when willing those shares the way he had—so that an impecunious suitor would become a wealthy man on the day he married her—was that that man might be more interested in marrying her for those shares than from love of her.

Not that Ryan was impecunious. He had been a wealthy man before their wedding day. He had... Oh, damn him! Damn him to hell, she thought angrily, and applied herself to her cleaning with renewed vigour.

'Fee-fi-fo-fum. I smell something delicious cooking,' Tessa said as, with her thin face serene from her day's work, she came in through the kitchen door that evening. Draping her jacket over a chair, she gave another appreciative sniff. 'Something, I should say, with a hint of...' she broke off. 'I say, have you been lacing whatever it is with polish?'

'I've *been* polishing,' Meredith confessed with a smile.

'So you've introduced yourself to my next-door neighbour,' quipped Tessa. 'Must have done—I'm sure I don't possess a tin of polish.'

'You don't—didn't. But I haven't borrowed any. I went to the shop in the village. Which reminds me—they know you have a guest.'

'They would,' Tessa said complacently. 'I told the milkman when I ordered extra milk.'

'Ah,' Meredith murmured, and asked, 'Do you want to eat now, or shall we wait and see if Aldo turns up?'

'Is there enough for three?'

'Ample,' Meredith replied.

'We'll wait awhile if you like. But since I only had a bar of chocolate for lunch, I'll have some bread and cheese to be going on with.'

Meredith knew her friend lost count of time when she was working, so together they made some sandwiches and a pot of tea, while Meredith made a mental note, if Tessa was going sketching again tomorrow, to pack her some sandwiches to take with her.

Drinking tea while her friend took the edge off her hunger, they talked idly of one thing and then another, with Tessa bringing Duncan's name into the conversation. 'He was so very special to me,' she said quietly, and while Meredith noted that the pain that had once been in her friend's voice when she spoke of Duncan had gone, Tessa went on to reveal, 'At one time, though, I thought I should never want to go out with any other man as long as I live—but that passed.'

'You've dated other men since Duncan died?' Meredith asked gently.

'A couple of times,' Tessa nodded. 'And it hasn't been anywhere near as bad as I expected.'

They fell into idle conversation again, then, as Meredith went to check that her efforts in the culinary department was not drying up in the oven as they waited to see if Aldo would come, Tessa went to have a wash and brush up.

Having checked the meal, Meredith returned to the kitchen table and, with her thoughts taken over entirely by Ryan, she was soon oblivious to her surroundings. Then Tessa silently returned.

'Perhaps he'll call,' she suggested gently.

'He won't,' Meredith replied, realising that she must have been staring into space, but not pretending that she didn't know whom Tessa was talking about. 'Apart from anything else,' she said, forcing a grin, 'he doesn't know where I am.'

But knowing for sure that she was never going to hear from Ryan Carlisle again did not stop Meredith's heart from going into her mouth when, not long afterwards, they heard a car draw up outside.

'Aldo, scorning the use of British Rail,' announced Tessa, and as she went to the door to let him in, sanity returned to Meredith

'Meredith!' her friend's brother exclaimed as he came into the kitchen, looking, to her eyes, older, sadder and wiser.

'How are you, Aldo?' Meredith smiled, finding that the hand she extended to shake his was taken, but also that he bent forward to plant a kiss of greeting on her cheek.

'Fine,' he replied, but it became very plain over their meal, when all he could talk of was Caroline and how she had walked out on him, that he was feeling far from fine.

Meredith was grateful to her friend that not a word did she say to indicate anything of her recent emotional upset. Though, since Aldo seemed to be suffering agonies, if not exactly in silence, Meredith doubted that he had any space for anyone else's problems.

At around ten, and just in case he wanted some private conversation with his sister, Meredith decided to go to bed. 'I'm afraid I've bagged the spare bedroom,' she told him, 'and...'

'And you have the honour of sleeping in the boxroom,' his sister chipped in. 'It's a bit cramped in there...'

'It doesn't matter,' he said, without much interest. 'I don't suppose I shall sleep anyway.'

Meredith went to bed vowing that for Tessa's sake she was going to be at her most cheerful in the morning. Not that she could remember going around with the long face which Aldo wore.

She was first up the next morning, and when Tessa came into the kitchen a short while later Meredith was bright and breezy as she said sunnily, 'I was going to bring you a cup of tea up.'

'Don't!' Tessa shuddered teasingly. 'I can't take such heartiness first thing in the morning!'

'Sorry,' Meredith smiled. 'Only it seemed to me that with both Aldo and me coming here and unburdening our . . .'

'Oh, for goodness' sake, Meredith!' Tessa cut her off. 'You're nothing at all like Aldo, if that's what's worrying you. Grief, part of his trouble is that he should have been an actor—surely you remember how dramatic he's always been about absolutely everything?'

'I must have fogotten,' Meredith murmured. 'But . . .'

'But nothing,' Tessa said firmly. 'You were here like a shot the time when I needed you, and I should be very hurt if you'd thought of going anywhere but here when you needed a bolt-hole. Besides,' she added, with a sudden smile, 'I like having you here.'

'If you put it like that,' Meredith smiled back, 'I'll—er—make the toast.'

They breakfasted together, with Tessa telling her wryly that, for all her dear brother had declared that he didn't suppose he would get any sleep, he must be finding the camp bed singularly comfortable.

When, as they cleared the table, Tessa went on to ask if she'd mind if she disappeared with her sketch-pad again that day, Meredith knew that they were true friends.

Having made some sandwiches for her to take, Meredith put them down on the corner of the solid kitchen dresser while Tessa got her things together.

'See you when the sun goes down,' grinned Tessa, and was off down the path, with Meredith chasing after her with the sandwiches Tessa had overlooked.

Meredith returned indoors with a trace of a smile about her mouth, realising again that, once Tessa had her mind on her work, she forgot about everything else. She hoped, though, that she would remember to eat.

Soon, though, Tessa had been replaced in her thoughts by Ryan. Knowing the futility of trying to keep him out of her head for very long, she let him stay as she washed the dishes and set the kitchen to rights.

He was still there in her head, and she was still trying to hate him, when she went into the sitting-room with her duster and did a general tidy around.

She was glad to see Aldo when, somewhere around eleven, he surfaced and came into the kitchen seeking a cup of coffee. She noticed his weak mouth for the first time, and wondered how on earth she had ever come to have had a crush on him, but she was still hopeful that conversation with him might take her mind off the man she had so foolishly married.

'How did you sleep?' she enquired out of politeness, and heard chapter and verse, interspersed with long, meaningful silences, about how insomnia was his soul-mate since Caroline had opted for pastures new.

Later on Meredith made him a snack lunch and listened while he talked 'Caroline' as she peeled potatoes and got everything ready for the evening meal.

She was brimful of Caroline, though, when at some time after three that afternoon the telephone in the hall rang. 'I'll get it,' she told Aldo quickly, and made her escape into the hall, knowing for sure that when it came to unburdening the soul, compared to Aldo she had been as if mute. Ready to take down any message for Tessa, Meredith went across to the telephone and picked it up. 'Hello,' she said. The wires seemed totally dead, for no one answered. 'I'm afraid Tessa's out,' she said, 'but...' The dialling tone in her ear told her that whoever was calling Tessa preferred to talk to her in person and had no wish to leave a message.

Putting the telephone back on its rest, Meredith took a deep breath and, on her way back to Aldo, she knew that, with the softest heart in the world, she could not take another basinful of 'Caroline'—not yet, anyway. Though if she took herself off for a walk, Aldo would no doubt suggest that he accompany her.

'I've got one or two jobs I want to do upstairs,' she popped her head round the door to tell him. 'Will you excuse me if...'

'I think I'll take a stroll—er—would you like to come with me?' he thought to ask.

'Oh, no, thank you, Aldo,' Meredith said quickly. 'I'll—er—I'll have a nice cup of tea waiting for you when you come back.'

His stroll did not take him long, but Meredith's strength had been renewed in his absence. Though at six o'clock she had formed the very definite view that if Aldo was staying longer than tomorrow, when next Tessa took herself off sketching, she was going to go with her.

Just then, though, she heard the sound of a car pulling up and, as relief entered her soul, she at first thought that it was Tessa returning. Somehow, though, this car sounded somewhat smoother than Tessa's car. When a short while later the front door bell rang, she knew positively that it was not Tessa.

But Meredith was ready to welcome their caller with open arms, whoever he or she might be, and she was first out of her chair as, with another, 'I'll get it,' this time she made for the front door.

Perhaps it was relief which was responsible for the smile she had on her mouth as she pulled back the door. But, even as her heart suddenly went crazy with joy, pride rocketed in to wipe the smile from her face. Because, though she had never expected to see him again, Meredith looked up and found herself staring straight into a pair of vividly remembered cool grey eyes.

Looking at him in disbelief, she recalled how she had told Tessa that the man she loved would not come calling because, quite simply, he did not know where she was. But the proof that he did know where she was was quite obvious as, striving hard for control, Meredith stared at none other than Ryan Carlisle.

She was still staring at him, solemn-faced, while her heart danced to see him, when that dance became a jig. For, even though his tone was as cool as his look, the words he smoothly spoke were, to her utter delight, the most beautiful words she had ever heard.

'Hello, Meredith,' he said. 'I've come for you.'

CHAPTER FOUR

MEREDITH'S wayward heart was singing. Ryan had come for her! He had just said so, which meant that there just had to have been a mistake somewhere. He must love her after all, she realised, and almost launched herself into his arms. Almost—but... Suddenly she was remembering the Burgess shares.

'You've—come for me?' she enquired, her tone cool as her common sense returned and she remembered in time how cool his tone had been. 'What on earth for?' she asked loftily, while her heart returned to a bitterly disappointed dull beat, and she wondered not only what all this meant, but how he had found her! 'There's nothing...'

'Your great-aunt rang,' Ryan cut her off shortly. 'Apparently her brother has been taken ill and...'

'Uncle Porter's ill!' Meredith exclaimed, although, in view of past experience of Uncle Porter, some of her alarm soon eased. She realised at once that this might be another instance of him playing to the gallery to get her to return to her old home, but even so, she knew that she could do no other than go to him. But, 'Why did my aunt ring you?' she asked Ryan snappily, refusing to slip back into the placid little mould she had inhabited before she had gone through a marriage ceremony with him.

'How the hell do I know?' he bit back, clearly not taken with this spirited young woman who seemed quite able to stand up for herself. Though his voice had changed, and had taken on a modicum of sarcasm when, silkily, he added, 'She probably rang me because you hadn't thought to let her have your forwarding address.'

She had not thought to let him have it either, Meredith thought crossly. But before she could ask him how he had found out where she was, she became aware that his glance had gone from her to somewhere over her shoulder.

Instinctively she looked back and, realising that she had forgotten all about Aldo, saw that he had come to see who she was talking to at the door. 'Er—this is Aldo Wallace,' she felt obliged to introduce him. 'Aldo,' she said, and, turning back to complete the introduction she saw that Ryan's eyes held chips of ice, and realised at once that he had no wish for her to introduce him as her husband. 'Aldo, this is Ryan Carlisle,' she said, having had no intention of telling Aldo that Ryan was her husband anyway. 'Come in, won't you?' she invited as suddenly Ryan's 'I've come for you' connected with him telling her that her great-uncle was ill. 'My uncle's ill,' she told Aldo as the three of them moved to the sitting-room, 'and Ryan has come to give me a lift to London.'

'Oh, I'm so sorry, Meredith,' Aldo said gently, and straight away offered, 'But I can drive you back to London. There's no need for...'

'There's no need for that,' Ryan cut him off curtly. 'I'll drive my wife to...'

'Wife!' Aldo exclaimed, and as he looked at Meredith in astonishment, and she coloured, for no reason other than that she experienced an absurd joy that Ryan was still referring to her as his wife. 'You never told me you were married!' Aldo added, and made it sound so much as if it meant something to him, and as if she should have told him the instant that she had greeted him yesterday, that Meredith felt the least Ryan would think was that the two of them were having some sort of an affair.

'There—was so much else to talk about,' she said weakly, and suddenly felt weaker still when all at once Ryan caught hold of her left hand.

'Had you used your eyes, Wallace,' he told him curtly, holding her hand in front of him, 'you'd have noticed that the lady wears a wedding ring.'

Abruptly Meredith snatched her hand back. She'd had enough! 'I'll go and get some things together,' she said shortly, and left them standing there.

Up in her bedroom, she packed her case and wished she'd had more about her than to sentimentally want to keep that wedding band on her finger. It meant nothing, for goodness' sake, and it was for certain that Ryan had not been sentimentally inclined when he had put that ring there.

She was about to take it off, just to show him that it did not matter, when she realised that he would notice its absence—just as he had spotted that she still wore it—and would most likely presume she had taken it off because of his reference to it.

Meredith carried her case downstairs with her wedding ring still on her finger. Her aunt, for one, would think her most odd if she was not wearing it when she saw her, and as yet, she realised that she was still not ready to tell her that her marriage was over.

'Will you tell Tessa that I'll phone her?' Meredith asked Aldo, as she found both men standing in the hall.

'Of course,' he answered, and, telling her that he hoped that things would be improved with her uncle when she saw him, he leaned forward and kissed her cheek. 'Bye, pet,' he bade her, and Ryan took her case in one hand and took a firm hold of her arm with the other, and escorted her out of the cottage.

'Where was your friend?' he asked as he set his car in motion.

'Out sketching,' Meredith replied. 'She went out early this morning.'

'Leaving you at home playing house with her brother,' Ryan stated—nastily, Meredith thought. 'I presume he's staying at the cottage too?'

'You presume correctly,' she told him stiffly, and spent the next silent half-hour sending hate vibes in his direction and wondering at the peculiarities of love, that she should hate him while she was with him, but not when she was apart from him.

After a half an hour of hating him, though, she was in love with him again. He need not have come up all the way to Derbyshire to collect her, yet he had. She had thought their parting final, but ... Suddenly, a thought occurred to her and she found herself breaking into speech in a flurry of panic.

'You didn't tell my great-aunt that we've separated, did you?' she asked, knowing full well that her aunt was going to be mightily upset, appalled and disbelieving at the news. And, although she was not ready yet to break that news to her, Meredith could see that it would be better if she led up to telling her gently rather than having Ryan tell her straight out, the way he most likely would.

'You clearly haven't told her,' he replied tersely.

'Have you?' Meredith snapped.

'No!' he answered shortly, but seemed to relent as he added, 'I wasn't certain what you wanted your aunt and uncle to be told, so I left it for the time being.'

'They'll have to be told when we divorce,' Meredith commented, her thoughts bleak on that future prospect.

'You've divorcing me?' Ryan asked, that short note swiftly back in his voice.

As she had not given divorce a moment's thought, but was not likely to tell him that, Meredith's voice was cool as she replied, 'When I get round to it.'

She soon realised, though, that Ryan was a man who liked to be the one in charge of things when, most aggressively, he snarled, 'It's to be hoped that I don't beat you to it!'

'What possible grounds have *you* got?' she demanded, her ire fired as, very far from placid, she rounded on him.

'I'd say that you refusing to sleep with me on our wedding night might be fairly strong grounds, wouldn't you?' he asked loftily, and Meredith was back to hating him again.

She turned and looked out of the window. As she remembered it—for all his comment that, 'It might have been interesting to teach you a few things', he hadn't shown any signs of being desperate to get her into his bed.

All was silent in the car again as Meredith fumed against him, worried about her great-uncle yet wondering if Uncle Porter was really so bad, since it had been Aunt Evelyn who had telephoned Ryan, and not Mrs Key.

'What exactly did my aunt say?' broke from her lips when she had been determined not to say another word.

'Little, except that her brother had suffered another of his turns, and that he wanted to see you.'

That sounded fairly normal and very like every other time she had been called home, Meredith considered. But, thinking of those times and how, barring the other time she had been at Tessa's when the call had come, she had been back home within the hour, she just had to ask, 'Were you—er—able to cover for my not being at your place? The thing is,' she went on quickly, 'my uncle's had these attacks before and I've always...'

'Breathe easy,' Ryan instructed. 'I explained to your aunt that, as I'd a full afternoon of paperwork in front of me, you'd gone shopping and might not be back for hours.'

'I—er—thank you,' Meredith said, and they were nearly in London when she gave way to a question, this time one that had been concerning her for some time now. 'How did you know where to find me?' she asked suddenly apropos of nothing. 'I didn't tell you where I was going, and...'

'There's no great mystery,' Ryan cut in. 'You'd spoken of your friend Tessa Wallace who lived in Derbyshire. When Preston expressed the hope as I left for my office on Tuesday that you'd made it to St Pancras in time to catch your train, it didn't take a master brain to work out where you'd gone.'

Meredith refrained from telling him that she'd had no thoughts of going to Derbyshire when she had taken a taxi to St Pancras railway station on Tuesday. But, as she took in how easily two and two always added up to four for this man she had married, she went on to dot a few 'i's and cross a few 't's as she tried a little adding up herself.

'So, having remembered my telling you that Tessa lived in a place called Little Haversham, you motored up and stopped at the village store to ask where she lived.' It was not a question but, as Meredith made the simple calculation, a statement. When Ryan made a small movement of his head to indicate her conclusions were at fault, though, she had to accept that her powers of deduction would never be as accurate as his.

'Your friend's name and address is in the phone book,' he tossed at her casually.

'Huh,' Meredith grunted, and was silent for all of five seconds when suddenly, in connection with the telephone, she remembered something. 'Did you ring Tessa's number just after three this afternoon?' she enquired.

'I saw no point in driving out of my way had I got my facts wrong,' he replied coolly.

'Why didn't you say something when I answered the phone, then?' Meredith asked—she thought it was a perfectly natural question. 'Why drive all that way, anyway?' she went on before he had answered her first question. 'You could just as easily have given me the message that my uncle was ill and I could have taken the next train to London or...'

'Or have got your friend's kissing brother to give you a lift,' Ryan said curtly.

Quite obviously, Ryan had not taken to Aldo, Meredith realised, and she supposed that beside her husband Aldo did show up as being rather weak. But Aldo was kind and, ignoring the fact that the man she had married had been kind too, to have gone very much out of his way to come to collect her, she instead preferred to believe that he had not put himself out at all on her behalf.

'No doubt you had business in Derbyshire anyway,' she said stiffly, and realised that for once she had got it right when, after a moment's pause, he replied,

'I—had, as a matter of fact. Little Haversham is a bit off the beaten track, which is why I rang first. The reason I didn't speak when you answered the phone,' he went on after another pause, 'was because to do so would have given you a few extra hours of worry in the intervening period before my calling for you.'

The knowledge that Ryan Carlisle had thought to save her a few extra hours of worry made Meredith warm to him. Though suddenly she remembered how he believed she had married him only because she just could not wait to leave her home. And all at once it came to her that she must show none of the warmth she felt for him, if he was not to suspect the true reason why she had married him. At the same moment, too, she realised that, for someone who could not wait to shake the dust of her old home from her heels, she had reacted far too quickly by going to pack her case within a very short space of him telling her that her uncle was ill.

'You—er—must have realised,' she said slowly, 'that—er—despite everything, I love my great-aunt and great-uncle very much.'

'Of course,' Ryan replied promptly, and Meredith began to like him as well as be in love with him, when he added, 'I care for my relatives too—but I wouldn't want to live with them.'

Meredith knew the instant she saw her great-aunt that there was nothing faked about this, her great-uncle's latest 'turn'. 'How is he?' she asked when, seeing her Aunt Evelyn looking worried and drawn, she went and put her arms around her.

'It's been a bad do, Meredith,' her aunt replied. 'Though he seems much better since Dr Hastings came and gave him an injection. He's still as stubborn as a mule, though, and has refused point-blank to go to hospital.'

Hospital! Meredith thought, starting to get seriously alarmed. There had never been any talk of Uncle Porter going into hospital before!

'I'll go and see him,' she said quickly. 'I'll . . .'

'He's asleep at the moment. Dr Hastings has told me that he should be all right now, but not to hesitate to give him a ring if I'm at all worried.'

Making a mental note to have a few words with Dr Hastings herself, Meredith saw that she would be calling the doctor to her aunt before long if she wasn't careful.

'Have you eaten at all today?' she asked her as she guided her into the sitting-room and sat her down.

'I couldn't,' her aunt replied.

'Didn't Mrs Key come in today?' asked Meredith, wondering why her aunt and not the cheerful treasure of a daily help had telephoned Ryan. The Mrs Key she thought she knew was the salt of the earth, and was much more likely to have stayed on and waited with her aunt than to have left her to fend for herself.

'Mrs Key's son came off his motorbike yesterday,' Aunt Evelyn explained. 'The poor woman, she went quite to pieces when her daughter-in-law rang here to tell her. Anyway, Michael's going to be quite all right, but Mrs Key had to have today off in order to babysit while Michael's wife spends some time at the hospital with him. Lilian, from next door,' she inserted for Ryan's benefit in case he had not remembered Mrs Peplow at the wedding, 'has been in on and off through the day.

It was Harold, her son,' she again inserted for Ryan's benefit, 'who helped the doctor get Porter to bed.'

Unable to leave her aunt, who seemed to have a need to talk, Meredith grew anxious in the next thirty minutes about preparing her a snack meal. Suddenly, though, she realised that, as her aunt appeared to have eaten nothing at all that day, there was every likelihood that Ryan had not eaten a bite since lunchtime either.

'I'm making a cheese omelette for my aunt, but I can put some steak under the grill for you if you prefer,' she told him when, since he had made no move to return to his apartment during the last half-hour, she guessed that perhaps he thought for her aunt's sake that he had better act out his husband's role.

'A cheese omelette sounds fine to me,' he replied, just as though he feared, rightly, that the steak would have to be grilled straight from the freezer. 'Can I help?' he asked.

Meredith realised that he, like she, had seen that now was the worst possible time for either of them to acquaint her aunt with the news that their marriage was over, and she supposed she was grateful to him that he was playing his role to the full.

She was not grateful to him an hour later, though. She had been upstairs to check on her uncle and had returned downstairs, having left a small light on in his bedroom. Then, coaxing her aunt to go to bed, saying that she would keep an eye on her uncle, Meredith added that she would not return to Ryan's apartment that night, but that she would stay at her old home for a day or two.

But no sooner had she helped her aunt up out of her chair than Evelyn Simmons was turning to Ryan and was saying, 'You'll stay too, of course, Ryan.' And while

Meredith, in sudden panic, was seeking an immediate excuse why he should not stay, her aunt was going on, 'I feel dreadful as it is that I interrupted your honeymoon the way I did. I shan't rest at all easy,' she declared, 'if I have to go to bed knowing that my actions have parted husband and wife.'

With nothing brilliant coming to Meredith in the way of a reason why Ryan should return alone to his home that night, she looked to him for help. To her dismay, though, not to say fury, he seemed to be in complete agreement that his place was under the same roof as his wife, and Meredith could cheerfully have killed him when he told her aunt, 'I can't have you uneasy on my account, Miss Simmons. Of course I'll stay.'

'But—but . . .' Meredith butted in, and when two pairs of eyes looked at her, one faded blue pair, and a pair of cool grey—and, if she was not very much mistaken, amused—ones, she prepared to lie her head off. 'But I've already pulled you away from your paperwork, Ryan,' she protested. 'I really don't think . . .'

'Don't give it another thought, darling,' he told her smoothly. 'I can get up early in the morning, and carry on with it then.' And, while she was silently fuming, You pig! just as though he did not know what she was thinking he calmly took over her job of aiding her aunt up the stairs. Trailing after them, Meredith heard her aunt telling him that it was a good job, with him being so tall and everything, that Meredith's bed was a large one.

Mutinying every step of the way, Meredith was just thinking that were her bed ten feet wide, she still would not be sharing it with Ryan Carlisle, when they came to her great-uncle's bedroom. Her aunt left them briefly as she went to take a look at her brother. She reported back that he was asleep and they went on along the landing to the last door but one, which was the door to Evelyn Simmons' room.

'Find Ryan something to sleep in, dear,' she requested as the three of them halted.

'Like a shroud,' Meredith muttered, too low for her aunt to hear, but she got the shock of her life when, as she bent to kiss her aunt, she saw the most terrific grin split Ryan's features.

Angrily, as her aunt's bedroom door closed, she marched back to the airing cupboard. It had not been her intention to amuse him! Extracting sheets, pillow slips and towels, in much the same way as last Saturday he had done for her, she added one extra item to the bundle—one of her uncle's nightshirts. She knew that Ryan was not going to wear it, but since her aunt had put in the request, who was she to argue? Then she went back towards him and went on to the end of the landing to her old room.

Mrs Key had been at work, Meredith saw as she entered, in that there was no trace at all that up until a week ago the room had been hers. Oddly, though, for all the mutiny in her heart, Meredith had no wish to return to live in her old home, or to take permanent possession of this room. She had grown up, she realised. Maybe the hurt Ryan had inflicted on her was responsible for that. Feeling the sting of tears at the backs of her eyes, she abruptly dropped the linen she was carrying down on the bed, and headed for the door.

To her consternation, however, Ryan was blocking the doorway. 'Excuse me,' she muttered, keeping her head well down.

'What's wrong?' he questioned, and Meredith wanted to hit him.

'You have to ask?' she snapped, knowing that if he had gleaned that she had been upset, he would put it down to her being worried about her uncle, but feeling mightily relieved all the same that she no longer felt like shedding a tear.

'Your aunt says this present crisis is over.'

'So I'll say goodnight,' Meredith hinted as he continued to block her path.

'Am I to take it you aren't sharing that bed with me?' Ryan asked, and, wanting to hate him, Meredith fell deeper in love with him at the laughter that danced in his eyes.

'What? And risk ruining your only chance to divorce me?' she mocked. Pushing past him, she went quickly before the weak person he could so easily make of her won the day.

Putting thoughts of Ryan from her, she went back along the landing to her uncle's room. To her surprise, he was awake. 'I thought I was going to die,' he complained in greeting, showing no wonder at seeing her there, but just accepting that, if he was ill, she would naturally return from wherever she was.

'They only take the good ones first,' she replied cheerfully.

'Sauce!' he snapped, then asked, 'Can I have a banana sandwich?'

She was ready to humour him in whatever he wanted. Even if she did consider that a banana sandwich—something she could never recall him eating before, and at midnight—might give him roaring indigestion.

'I'll go and make you one,' she told him. 'Close your eyes and rest while I've gone.'

Going quietly to the kitchen, Meredith mashed all the indigestible lumps out of a banana and, adding a sprinkling of sugar to give him energy and on account of his sweet tooth, she made her uncle a sandwich and returned upstairs with it, to discover that he had fallen asleep again.

Finding a large handkerchief in one of his drawers, she covered the plate and put it down on his bedside table. Then she quietly pulled a chair up to his bed and settled herself down. Poor love, he could be as cantankerous as the devil when the mood was on him, but she could see his veins through the paper-thin skin on his face—and, cantankerous or no, she loved him.

For the next three hours Meredith kept a watching eye on her uncle while her thoughts floated to the other man she loved. Though, she realised, she was more in love with Ryan than loving him. True, she had today discovered that she was beginning to like him—something which there had been no time to discover, or even think about, during their whirlwind courtship—if courtship was the word.

Meredith felt good inside as she recalled how she had seemed to amuse him. She enjoyed seeing him amused; she loved that look in his eyes when all his habitual coolness disappeared. He had been kind too. So what if he had had business in Derbyshire? he need not have taken on the responsibility—adding extra miles on to his trip—of calling for her to bring her back to London.

She had thought she would never see him again, yet he had known, before she had, where she would be. But, since he had known he would find her in Little Haversham, and had confirmed that by ringing Tessa's number, he could easily have given her the bad news over the telephone. But he had not. Really, Meredith considered, the man she had married was rather a nice person.

'What are you looking so smitten about?'

Her tender thoughts were rudely interrupted by her uncle who, unbeknown to her, had wakened a minute earlier and had lain watching her. Swiftly she changed course, to concentrate solely on a different male.

'Have a banana sandwich,' she suggested, only to find that he had woken in a crotchety mood and had gone off the idea of a banana sandwich.

'I'd like a cup of tea,' he announced.

Suspecting that he would be asleep again by the time she got back, Meredith hurried on tiptoe to the kitchen. While the kettle boiled she set a tray for two, and added some sweet biscuits, and a short while later she was returning up the stairs.

'How did you get here?' her great-uncle asked as she adjusted his pillows when he said he wanted to sit up.

'Ryan brought me,' she replied, swinging his mobile bed table round in front of him and placing his tea and biscuits down on it.

'Where's Ryan now?' he wanted to know.

'Asleep—in my old room,' Meredith told him, and added quickly, 'There's nothing seriously wrong with you. I'm sitting with you because I couldn't sleep, and so came to see how you were.'

'You usually go to bed in your day clothes?' he grunted, seventy-seven and as alert as ever he had been.

'Are you going to drink that tea or not?' Meredith, with no answer, put a question.

'Marriage has made a bossy woman out of you,' her uncle complained, and, just as she was going to apologise, 'I want to play chess,' he demanded.

Was there ever such a cantank...? Meredith remembered how she was going to humour him. 'Drink your tea first,' she suggested.

Just before seven, someone else walked into the bedroom, saw two figures asleep over a chessboard, and smiled.

Something touching her forehead brought Meredith awake. She looked up and saw her tall husband smiling down at her.

'Did you—did you kiss me?' she asked, something in her sleep-befuddled brain telling her that he had.

Ryan put a warning forefinger to his lips and looked to where her great-uncle slept on. 'I'm just off,' he told her in a low voice, and, as Meredith wondered why he should kiss her goodbye for her uncle's benefit when her uncle was asleep, she came fully awake to realise, with inner dismay, that Ryan was leaving.

'I'll see you out,' she whispered, and rising from her chair, she ignored the fact that sleeping in a bedside chair had made her ache in several places at once, and went with him down the stairs and along the hall to the front door. 'Thank you for—yesterday,' she told him politely when, wanting to do anything to delay his leaving, she stamped down the suggestion that she should cook him a man-size breakfast before he went anywhere.

'Any time,' he said and, looking down at her, he smiled, and because she liked his smile Meredith found she could do no other than smile back. And then joy was in her fast-beating heart, for with muttered words which sounded like, 'What a delight you are!' suddenly Ryan was reaching for her. 'Come here, Meredith Carlisle,' she heard him say more distinctly, 'and give your husband the time-honoured farewell.'

There was no thought in her head, as she thrilled to hear him call her by her new surname—his surname— to refuse to do as he bade. She had grown to like this man whose well-shaped mouth was now over hers. Her arms went up and around him. He was a nice man, a kind man, and she was in love with him.

Warmly Ryan kissed her, and as Meredith clung to him, his arms tightened about her. Then their kiss came to an end and, as Meredith tried with limited success to grab a cloak of sense about her, Ryan put her from him. His eyes stayed riveted to her eyes for about a second, then moved to take in her shy face and still-parted lips. Then, as if he needed some sort of control, he reached for the door-catch, glancing back, not at her, but briefly over her shoulder.

Then, as she tried not to let him see that there was a person inside her who wanted to implore him not to leave, so without another word he went from her.

Meredith stood stock-still when the door had closed after him. Just as she somehow felt that Ryan had been unable to stop himself from taking her in his arms and kissing her, so she had felt unable to do anything but respond to him when he had kissed her. And, just then, she did not regret that he could not have been unaware of her response to him.

Feeling forlorn that he had gone, Meredith turned, but, as she took one small pace back along the hall, she suddenly froze on the spot. For there, watching her, as she must have watched both her and Ryan sharing what must seemed a loving farewell, stood her aunt—and suddenly Meredith hated Ryan Carlisle.

Because he wasn't nice, and he wasn't kind, and he was a pig! Because she loved him and he didn't love her, and she had kissed him from love and he—he had only kissed her because he had known that her aunt had been watching.

CHAPTER FIVE

On and off throughout that morning, Meredith ran up and down the stairs fetching this, that or the other which her tetchy male relative demanded. But no matter how demanding her uncle was, or how irritable in his recovery, it did not stop her from thinking what a rat Ryan Carlisle was.

She was positive, as she carried a breakfast tray up the stairs, that Ryan had known her aunt had been in the hall *before* he had pulled her into his arms. She grew more annoyed when she thought of how she had determined that never again would he play her for a fool. So where had her brains been when his lips had met hers?

Meredith was taking a mid-morning warm drink up to her uncle when, unable to get out of her mind the willing way she had responded, she recalled again the idiotic way she had believed Ryan had been searching for some sort of control when he had glanced back over her shoulder and along the hall. For goodness' sake, as if she did not have enough proof of what a double-dyed rat he was! He had *known* her aunt was there! His glance had been merely to confirm that her aunt had observed the newlyweds taking fond leave of each other!

She was hurrying down the road to get the Sunday papers and some of her uncle's favourite 'Army and Navy' tablets when the obscure reason why Ryan should want her aunt to witness their 'lovers' parting became clear. Quite plainly he had seen to it that, were she now to tell Aunt Evelyn what a monster he had been over those shares, her dear old-fashioned aunt would smile and say, 'Well, you've obviously forgiven him, dear.'

The smooth-talking rodent, he knew perfectly well how very difficult she was going to find it to tell her family that her marriage was over! By kissing her—and, dammit, getting her full response—he had ensured that to tell her they had separated would be more impossible than merely difficult.

Meredith was coming back from the paper shop when the answer why he should want to make things so impossible for her broke through. Despite his telling her that she was her own person now, he had not liked it when she'd told him she would divorce him when she got round to it. Quite patently, he wanted any decision about divorce to be his prerogative alone.

Chauvinistic devil! she fumed; he was so used to being top dog that it was totally alien to him to allow any female to decide on anything which involved him. No female was going to tell him she would divorce him—*he* would make the decision as to when they would divorce.

She began to cool down when, as she was about to cross the road by the telephone box near to her old home, she suddenly realised that she would be more able to speak freely to Tessa if she rang her from the coin-box rather than the family sitting-room.

'Hello, Tessa, it's Meredith,' she said a few minutes later.

'How are things?' Tessa asked quickly. 'Your uncle—was it another of his false alarms?'

'It was more serious this time,' Meredith replied, and went on to reveal how Dr Hastings had wanted him to go into hospital, but how her uncle had refused. 'Uncle Porter is being particularly crotchety this morning,' she confided, 'so I'm hoping that that's a good sign that he's returning to normal.' Then she went on to speak of her aunt and of a few domestic matters, and then, and because Tessa was her very good friend and would not intrude unless invited, she enquired, 'I suppose Aldo told you that Ryan arrived to give me a lift?'

'That was—kind of him,' commented Tessa, sounding determined not to pry.

'He was in the area on business anyway,' Meredith told her, 'so it was no particular hardship for him to make a detour to Little Haversham,' and because she just couldn't help it, '...the rat,' she added.

'Which means that you still love him,' Tessa said gently.

Meredith returned to take the papers and her uncle's favourite sweets up to him, with her head full of this crazy business called love. How was it that, even when she knew her love for the swine he was, she should still love him? Logically, having learnt what she had, as instantly as she had fallen *in* love with Ryan she should have as instantly fallen *out* of love with him.

She sighed to herself as she prepared a light lunch in the kitchen. That was the trouble with falling in love— there was no logic in it.

Dr Hastings looked in shortly after lunch to see how his patient was, and, showing him up to her uncle's room to save her elderly aunt's legs, Meredith answered the doctor's questions pertinent to his condition, and asked a few of her own.

Allowing her uncle his privacy, she waited on the landing outside when the doctor went in. Her uncle's heart was growing weaker, he had told her, but with modern medicines he could go on for years yet.

'Is he always so charming?' Dr Hastings asked as he came from the room and together they went down the stairs.

At first Meredith thought the doctor was being sarcastic, but one quick glance at his face showed that his question was genuine and, as she realised that her uncle had chosen to give his seldom-seen angelic side an outing, loyalty to her aged relative made her say, 'He—er—can be a trifle—er—not so charming occasionally.'

A few minutes later she had understood that her uncle was much improved and could get up tomorrow. He could, Dr Hastings had said, carry on exactly as before, with the exception that it might be better if she could make a bedroom for him downstairs.

'Well, that's no problem, is it, Aunty?' Meredith said when she had seen the doctor out. And, being cheerful for her aunt's sake, 'We've ample room down here and...'

'Too much room, if you ask me,' Evelyn Simmons stated. 'This house is too big for Porter and me now that you've gone,' and before Meredith could get in a hint that she might be coming back she went on, 'I thought it too big while you lived with us, for that matter. There are so many rooms we don't use, and which have to be kept aired and heated. It's such a waste of good money.'

Meredith, who knew the ins and outs of their income well, knew that, although they were not in any way near as well off as they had been thirty years ago, her aunt spoke more from a feeling of thrift than from penury.

But, realising that since her aunt had been born and brought up in this large old house she had therefore absolutely no intention of leaving it, and was just letting off gentle steam, Meredith left the subject there.

'I think I'll go and get the vegetables cleaned ready for dinner,' she told her aunt, making her way to the door.

'I'll come and help,' Evelyn Simmons said, and although it had been Meredith's idea for her great-aunt to put her feet up for a while, she gave in gracefully. Whether Uncle Porter's being ill had anything to do with it she did not know, but it seemed to her that, as her great-aunt grew older, so she grew more independent.

Having spent most of the morning drumming up her hate against Ryan Carlisle, Meredith had simmered down and her equilibrium was far calmer than it had been as in the kitchen she chopped and inspected cabbage while her aunt peeled potatoes. Suddenly, though, her aunt dropped a question into the companionable silence, and in doing so, shattered Meredith's equilibrium entirely.

'Is Ryan coming to dinner?' she asked innocently.

'What . . . ?' Startled, Meredith glanced at her quickly.

'You were dreaming,' her aunt teased, noting her startled look, and, smiling, she explained, 'I need to know if I should peel more potatoes than I normally do.'

'Oh! No! Er—that's fine, Aunty,' Meredith babbled. Then, getting herself more collected, outwardly at least, 'Ryan's got so much paperwork to catch up on . . .' she invented hastily, '. . . that he—er—won't want to break off to eat.'

Her aunt tut-tutted a little at the very idea of a man of Ryan's build not breaking off from work to stop for a three-course meal. But, having invented his 'fast' on the spur of the moment, Meredith had more serious things to think about. Suddenly she was battling to conceal her panic at the notion her aunt had just triggered off. Because, with Ryan Carlisle turning out to be a far more complex man than she had believed, she had no idea if he might not only decide to come and join them for dinner but—with his nerve—decide to stay the night as well!

Blaming the fact that she had been so busy railing against him for her not having seen this possible eventuality until her aunt had prompted it, Meredith quieted her panic by coming to a firm resolve. While anything was possible where Ryan Carlisle was concerned, and she had learned the hard way not to put anything past him, she was most definitely not going to share her bed with him. She fully realised that, with her uncle improving, she had no excuse for sitting up with him again tonight and so keeping away from her bed, but if she had to sleep on the landing outside her room that night, she would.

It did not come to that, however. While part of Meredith was too honest not to acknowledge the fact that she was aching for a sight of him, the proud and *un*biddable side that had been awoken in her began to relax when dinnertime came and went with no sign of him.

Going upstairs to collect her uncle's used dishes, she accepted, having realised there was no logic where love was concerned, that relief and regret about not seeing Ryan were bound to mingle.

She spent a few minutes with her uncle, listening to his complaints—the potatoes were floury and he hated cabbage—and trying to jolly him along, then, promising to return later to give him a game of chess, she took his tray to the kitchen and washed up. Checking that the kitchen was spick and span, she went to the sitting-room, intending to keep her aunt company for half an hour before she returned upstairs.

'Did Porter eat his dinner?' her aunt asked as she went in.

'Under protest,' she smiled. 'I . . .' She broke off as the phone rang. Since they did not receive too many phone calls, Meredith's heart went wild, but she was the nearest to her uncle's chair, so she went to answer it. 'Hello,' she said, just knowing that she was being stupid and that it was probably a wrong number, or Tessa, or Mrs Peplow next door. But the absolutely super voice of Ryan Carlisle came down the wires and Meredith was all relief—with not a scrap of regret in sight.

'I thought that, for appearances' sake, you'd like me to phone,' he said urbanely.

A smile started somewhere deep inside her. 'I'm—glad you did,' she told him, and realised that her tone must have been much too warm, though fortuantely he had found a different reason for that warmth.

'Your aunt's within earshot, I take it?' he enquired, and Meredith rapidly pulled herself together.

'Uncle Porter is much improved,' she stated, as she answered his question by making believe he had just made an enquiry after her great-uncle's health.

'So tell me . . .' Ryan began, and while Meredith expected him to say something along the lines of him hoping her uncle's improvement continued, he caused her to flounder when—quite outrageously, she thought— he enquired, '. . . why wouldn't you sleep with me last night? The warmth of your response when we kissed this morning belies the fact that you hate me.'

Meredith was aware that her colour was high from his remarks, but although she recognised that, even should their marriage be consummated, Ryan, the clever devil, would soon find some grounds to divorce her when he was ready, the newly awakened unbiddable side of her was coming to the fore.

'Of course I'll be all right,' she entirely ignored his tormenting observations to reply. 'I've known for ages that you have to catch a plane tonight and will be away for at least two weeks.' She noted her aunt's quick look of surprise as she overheard this piece of news, and she managed to inject an artificially warm note into her voice when she felt forced, for her aunt's benefit, to add, 'I'll—er—be home waiting for you when you come back.'

'And where—lying baggage—will you be if I come back in under two weeks?' Ryan drawled, and even as she thought that he seemed amused by her strong hint that he should keep away for two weeks, it registered that he was saying that he would, regardless, still turn up tomorrow if he felt like it.

'Goodnight—darling,' she said, and put the phone down.

'I didn't know Ryan was going away tonight!' Evelyn Simmons exclaimed the moment Meredith looked up.

'Didn't I say?' she hedged.

Her aunt shook her head, but Meredith wanted to crawl away into a hole when suddenly her aunt smiled understandingly, and observed, 'I should have guessed when I saw you hugging each other so tightly this morning that you knew you weren't going to see each other for a couple of weeks.'

In no time at all Meredith's great-uncle Porter was up and about. On Monday Harold Peplow dropped in with some magazines for her uncle, and it was with his help, and that of Mrs Key, that Meredith moved her uncle's bed downstairs. Her uncle grumbled, of course, but he otherwise seemed pleased with all the fuss.

On Tuesday Meredith did the washing. On Wednesday, she ironed it. On Thursday she did the shopping, and on Friday she and Mrs Key gave several of the rooms a good spring-cleaning. And on Saturday, when Meredith realised she was wishing she had never pretended that Ryan would be away for two weeks, she faced the knowledge that she was yearning to see him.

Sunday dawned dull and desolate, and when not so much as a wrong number disturbed the phone bell that day she realised that Ryan, having taken her hint, was behaving honourably and would not be contacting her. And Meredith did not like it one bit.

Who was he, that he should start acting honourably *now*? All that day, she tried to whip up anger against him. But when she went to bed that night Meredith had seen that it was not so much that Ryan was acting honourably, but more that he had better things to do with his time than to remember her.

Having slept badly, she got up on Monday and knew an urge to get away. Her thoughts strayed to Tessa and to Little Haversham, and suddenly Meredith knew that, if Aldo was back in London, she would very much like to return to Derbyshire.

Uncle Porter was back to normal now, and she thought the matter through as she bathed and dressed. Mrs Key's son Michael was well on the mend from his motor-cycling accident; Mrs Key was back in full harness and, as well as being more than willing to keep an eye on her relatives, was more than able to cope with any crisis which might arise.

The idea of returning to stay with Tessa had taken root by the time Meredith went down the stairs. The idea was still buzzing around in her head as she and her aunt prepared the breakfast. And, by the time breakfast was over and her great-uncle Porter had taken himself off to the sitting-room with his newspaper, Meredith just had to say something on the subject.

'Would you mind very much if I went and stayed with Tessa for a while?' she asked her aunt as they loaded the trolley to be wheeled back to the kitchen.

'You're missing Ryan, of course,' her aunt pinpointed, and surprised Meredith slightly when she added, 'I've noticed how restless you've been ever since he went away,' and with not so much as a sign of a sharp note in her voice when she spoke of Tessa—which was more usual ever since Tessa had lived with her Duncan out of wedlock, 'You go, dear. Tessa will be pleased to see you, I feel sure,' she said in gentle understanding.

Unable to speak openly on the phone about the last time she had stayed with her, when Meredith rang Tessa to ask if she could come and stay, she added, 'If you're on your own?'

'I haven't seen anything of Aldo for over a week,' Tessa laughed, and sounded delighted at the prospect of having her to stay again.

Meredith took the train to Derbyshire the next day, and Tessa was at the station to meet her and was every bit as pleased to see her as Evelyn Simmons had said.

'Things at home still the same?' Tessa enquired as they drove along, having heard from Meredith the day before about her great-uncle's recovery.

'Pretty much,' Meredith replied. 'Uncle played up a bit when I told him I was coming away, but Aunt Evelyn told him I'd be going anyway when Ryan returned from abroad.'

'He's overseas?'

'No,' Meredith replied, and explained how she had let her aunt believe that Ryan had flown abroad on business.

'How's Aldo?' she asked, to change what was a painful subject.

'Between you and me—driving me up the wall!' Tessa replied.

'He's still heartbroken over Caroline?'

'That's just it!' Tessa exclaimed. 'After giving you, I suspect, as well as me a wretched time of it over his ex—blow me if he didn't ring up last night—as happy as Larry, mark you—to ask if he could bring his new girlfriend to meet me.'

'He didn't!' Meredith gasped stunned, and as both she and Tessa burst out laughing, she added, 'The stinker!' Having recovered, though, she was serious when she asked, 'So he and his girlfriend are coming to stay this weekend?'

'They are not!' Tessa said firmly. 'Love him dearly though I do, that brother of mine is fine in small doses only.'

At Tessa's cottage, Meredith took her case up to the room she had used before. Then she went downstairs, where she and her friend spent a relaxing afternoon talking of nothing in particular, but nevertheless still finding plenty of things to discuss.

Because Tessa was filling in for one of the art teachers at evening classes who had gone off sick, they dined early. 'You're sure you don't mind me leaving you on your first night here?' Tessa checked before she went.

'For heaven's sake,' Meredith told her, 'I wouldn't have come if I thought I was going to disrupt things for you. Besides, I'm dying to start that book you've loaned me.'

'Oh, well, if you put it like that!' Tessa smiled. 'I'll see you later.'

Ryan was back in Meredith's head the moment the door had closed after her friend. He was still there an hour later, the book Tessa had lent her to read still unopened on her lap. Ryan was much in her mind as she went over yet again how, when she had overheard him in conversation with Monte Montgomery on her wedding day, her world had fallen apart. Her chin had tilted at an angry angle as she relived hearing Ryan state, 'It's a bonus, of course, that she's a biddable little thing', when she was suddenly startled out of her thoughts by hearing the phone ring.

Not knowing who might be calling, but not feeling apprehensive that it might be Aldo ringing his sister for a chat—Caroline must be a lady of the past now—Meredith went to answer Tessa's phone.

'Hello,' she said, and straight away received an earful from, by the sound of it, a very irate husband!

Ryan's voice, though still as fabulous as she had always thought it, was right now at its most disagreeable. 'What the hell do you think you're doing in Derbyshire?' he roared down the line.

'You—r-rang my home?' she queried, rendered almost speechless at hearing him so entirely unexpectedly.

'I rang your aunt pretending to be calling you from abroad,' he rapped furiously. 'The least you could have done was to let me know your movements!' And, while Meredith began to get over her astonishment at hearing from him so surprisingly, fairly violent emotions—prodded by her recent memory of him referring to her as 'A biddable little thing'—began to stir in her. 'Don't expect me to go in to bat for you if...' he barked.

'I never asked you to go in to bat for me!' a very unbiddable Meredith hurled spiritedly back at him.

'You sure as hell don't want it broadcast that our marriage is over!' he bellowed, and slammed down the phone before she could think of a suitable answer.

Swine! she fumed, and refused to cry. Pig, pig, pig, she silently berated him, but it was rather weakening to know that he could not be such a total swine, or else why would he have realised that her aunt might well have begun to wonder that he had not been in touch, and rung pretending to her that he was ringing from abroad?

It came to Meredith over the next few days that the time was drawing closer when she would have to confess to her aunt and uncle that her marriage was over. Somehow, though, no matter how many ways she thought up to explain to them the way it was, she never once thought of telling them the true reason why she and Ryan would not be living under the same roof. She was still thinking of the peculiarity of love on Friday, in that, while *she* could call Ryan a pig, and anything else that came to mind, she just found it beyond her to blacken his name to her aunt and uncle.

She and Tessa were sitting in the kitchen that evening, where the light was better, while Tessa practised her portrait skills for a village fund-raising event, when Tessa asked, 'Can I have a smile?' as her hand flew over her sketch-pad.

'Sorry,' Meredith apologised, and did her best to comply, even if she felt in not a very smiling mood as she cogitated on how best to break the news to her elderly relatives who believed that a marriage was forever.

'How's that?' asked Tessa as she tore the top piece of paper off her pad and handed it to her.

'Why, it's brilliant!' Meredith exclaimed, as she stared at the likeness of herself which her friend had just sketched. 'You'll make heaps for charity if you make all your sitters seem as carefree and full of life as you've made me look,' she said, as she glanced again at the drawing of the young woman who laughed back at her.

'It's more how I remember you looking when we were at art college,' Tessa told her as she took the charcoal-drawn portrait from her and studied it herself. 'It's how you'll look again, too, I've every confidence,' she told her.

'I can't wait!' Meredith grinned.

Later, when she went to bed, she could not help but wonder—would she? Somehow it seemed years away since she had last felt carefree. Yet it did not take her long to recall that the last time she had felt as carefree as that portrait had been that heady time when she had thought Ryan loved her.

'This morning,' Tessa announced at breakfast, 'I shall do some cleaning.'

'If you're serious, and with due respect I hardly believe my ears,' Meredith laughed, 'then I'll help.'

Tessa grinned as she detailed Meredith to 'do' the sitting-room while she herself 'sterilised' the kitchen. An hour later, though, Tessa had had more than enough and called through to the sitting-room, 'Shall we break for coffee?'

'It's only ten o'clock,' Meredith pointed out.

'Stick-in-the-mud!' Tessa jibed.

'Black or white?' responded Meredith as she went through to the kitchen to put the kettle on.

Tessa, although she tried hard, lost heart after that, and resumed work only briefly when she again called through to the sitting-room.

'I can do housework when it rains,' she said, and as Meredith joined her she began, 'The sun's shining,' but did not have to add more.

'Why don't you go and finish that bit of sketching you told me just wouldn't come right?' Meredith encouraged her. 'Perhaps you'll have better luck today.'

'Would you mind?'

'Of course not!'

'Come with me, then.'

Meredith thought of the books ready for dusting and which were temporarily all over the floor from her emptying the bookcase. 'Another time,' she told Tessa, and would have seen about making her some sandwiches to take with her, but her friend stopped her.

'If it all goes right, I should be through in about an hour,' she said, and made Meredith promise to cease all housework once she had the sitting-room back to rights. 'For my conscience's sake,' she pleaded.

'See you later,' Meredith called as she waved her off.

'I won't be long this time, I promise,' Tessa called as she got into her car. Meredith smiled—she had heard that before.

Once she had finished the sitting-room, and feeling a little grubby, she went and showered and changed into a full-skirted cotton dress. No matter what she did, though, Ryan kept her company.

When she was going to get him out of her head she had no idea, for he accompanied her to the general store when she decided to go and see what the store's refrigeration department had that might be interesting for dinner.

Returning from the general store, she made herself a lunchtime sandwich and a cup of coffee, and wondered what he was doing and where he was having his lunch.

She tried, without success, to oust him from her thoughts, but he refused to budge. He was still in her head an hour and a half later when she happened to glance out of the sitting-room window. And it was then that she thought that such constant thinking of him must have sent her over the edge, because she could have sworn she had just seen his car pull up outside.

Grief! she thought, as her heartbeat quickened, and, very much annoyed with herself, she took herself off to the kitchen. She would not give in to the temptation to go and look out of the sitting-room window a second time—she would not.

She had just set the kettle to boil for a cup of tea she had no particular interest in when a ring sounded from the front door bell, and suddenly everything in her went catastrophic.

It must have been his car! she thought. Only to at once counteract that thought by telling herself sternly not be ridiculous, there was more than one sleek black limousine around.

She was still having an inner argument when, with no idea of what she was going to say to him should it indeed prove to be Ryan and not wishful thinking—for in truth, she was aching for a sight of him—she went and answered what seemed a very impatient second ring at Tessa's front door.

'Oh, hello!' Meredith was inwardly delighted with herself that she had achieved such a surprised and even-sounding greeting.

'I thought you weren't in!' Ryan retorted uncivilly.

'I was in the kitchen,' she replied by way of explanation, rather than let him glean any idea of how she had gone to pieces when his first ring of the doorbell had sounded. 'Which reminds me,' she said, realising that she did not have to explain a thing, 'I've left the kettle boiling its head off. Er—come in,' she added, as she turned from him and made a dive for the kitchen.

'You're about to have a cup of tea?' he asked. Having switched the kettle off, Meredith looked at him and, spotting lines of tiredness around his eyes, went utterly weak.

'Would you like one?' she had offered before she had given herself time to think that it might be better if he made this visit as brief as possible.

'Thanks,' he accepted.

Meredith was not entirely sure how she felt at having him watching her as she warmed the teapot and popped in some teabags. 'If you'd like to take a seat in the sitting-room,' she hinted, and felt her ire start to rise when clearly he wanted to do nothing of the kind.

'What's wrong with the kitchen?' he enquired, and, as if hell-bent on watching her prowess as teamaker-in-chief, he pulled out a chair from beneath the kitchen table and sat looking on while she poured boiling water on the teabags.

Determined not to invite him to the sitting-room again, she set two cups of tea down on the kitchen table and pulled out a chair for herself at the other side. 'I expect you're this way on business?' she queried. But, remembering that the last time he had been in Derbyshire on business he had combined that trip with a detour to Little Haversham to tell her that her great-uncle was ill, she felt a sudden anxiety about her uncle.

Her anxiety was quickly quieted however when, with no sign of urgency Ryan drawled, 'I come this way once a year to visit a distant elderly relative on her birthday.'

'You've an elderly relative living...' this way, she would have ended, had he given her the chance, but, aggressive suddenly, Ryan had cut in to demand,

'Did you suppose you held exclusive rights in all elderly relatives?'

'No,' Meredith answered shortly. 'But you never told me about yours! Had you done so,' she went on a trace sarcastically, 'I'd have invited her to our wedding.'

'In the circumstances, it's just as well that she's too frail to travel!' Ryan tossed back at her caustically. And, while Meredith was feeling a rebirth of her recent face-slapping tendencies, he asked sharply, 'Where's your friend?'

'Tessa's out sketching!' Meredith snapped, nettled.

'And your other friend?' he barked abruptly.

'Other friend?' she queried curtly, not at all with him.

'Wallace, of the "Aldo and I" fame—the brother,' he elucidated in three different ways so that she could not help but know who he meant.

'He doesn't live here,' she retorted sourly, not liking the implication that she was dim not to know straight away who he meant. 'Aldo lives and works in London,' she added waspishly.

'So you haven't seen him this trip?'

With any other man, Meredith might have thought there was a suggestion of jealousy behind the question. But, since she knew little of men except one in particular—the one she had married—and the idea that he might be jealous was laughable, she kept her head, biting out, 'No, I haven't!' And when suddenly, and to her immense surprise, Ryan burst out laughing, she challenged hostilely, 'What's so funny?'

'It struck me that we sounded like some long-married couple,' Ryan answered. More because she preferred him in this better humour, Meredith had to smile—and then he made every one of her nerve-ends tingle when he gently touched a forefinger to the curving corner of her mouth, and murmured, half to himself, 'When did I ever consider you biddable?'

Such was his charm then that Meredith's backbone melted, and as she raised her eyes from his warm, smiling mouth to his warm grey eyes, she just could not keep a guard on her tongue. 'You look tired,' she told him.

'That's probably because I've been deskbound all week,' he replied.

'You find it more—stimulating—to be—er—up and doing, rather than locked behind your desk?' she queried, loving the fact that, for the first time ever, Ryan was allowing her to see a little of what made him tick.

'Much prefer it,' he answered openly, and, after a moment's pause, 'Which is why it was a pleasure to drive this way today.'

Meredith knew for sure that he could not be implying that he had found it a pleasure to drive to see her. Particularly she knew it when she recalled easily that his reason for being in Derbyshire that day was to visit an elderly relative. Knowing that, however, made it no easier to bear that she, his wife, must be an afterthought. Which, in turn, was perhaps responsible for her tone being a little tart when she told him, 'Riding around the country in a car isn't going to do you any good! What you need is some exercise in the fresh air.'

'You're suggesting we go for a walk?' he returned before she could blink.

'I wasn't, actually,' she said on a gasp.

'It's turned a mite chilly; you'll need a jacket,' he said, as if it was all settled.

'Are you this bossy at the office?' she countered, but she knew she would walk to the ends of the earth with him if he asked her—and that was before he smiled.

'Please,' he charmed her, and Meredith went to collect her jacket.

She thought she would never forget the enchantment of that walk. She later calculated that they were away from the cottage for about an hour. During that hour, though, she felt more at one with Ryan than she had ever been as they discussed any subject—barring their two selves—that came up.

Sadly, though, the harmony of that walk was not to last. They had turned round and were almost back at Tessa's cottage when Meredith, while marvelling at how in tune she and Ryan seemed to be, thought through a recent idea out loud. It went along the lines of her maybe renting a flat, and getting herself a permanent job.

'You're saying that, having made the break from your relatives, you now want to be totally independent?' Ryan queried, a dark frown coming to his good-looking features.

Meredith had not fully worked out her idea yet, but as it was burned on her brain that Ryan thought she had only married him to get away from her relatives, she was not going to disabuse him of the idea now.

'What's wrong with that?' she challenged him, and did not care that his frown deepened not only at her words but also her far from docile tone.

'I've already told you that I'll provide for you,' he told her sharply as they reached the cottage gate and stood glaring at each other, with Meredith suddenly cancelling out any notion she might have had to invite him in for some refreshment, and Ryan looking as though she'd have been wasting her breath anyway because the only place he was going was back to London. 'Where do you bank? I'll...'

'I don't need you to provide for me!' she flared hotly. 'I'm quite capable of...'

'It's my right to provide for you,' he cut her off bluntly. 'I have a duty to...'

'Good grief!' Meredith cut him off this time, her new-found temper getting well out of control that he, this man she loved with all her being, should consider her a 'duty'. 'Really, Ryan,' she mocked, surprising herself as much as him that her obedient self could sound so arrogant, 'you're just too old-fashioned for words!'

'Why, you little...' he began, and Meredith had a feeling that he was close to wanting to put his hands round her throat and throttle her. Only instead, some movement behind her caught his attention, and as she turned to see what it was she saw Tessa hurrying urgently down the path towards them.

Meredith's temper disappeared instantly when, without waiting for the niceties of introductions, Tessa said, 'Mrs Key's been on the phone, Meredith. Your uncle's been taken ill again—and this time it looks pretty bad.'

CHAPTER SIX

MEREDITH was grateful, as Ryan's car sped nearer and nearer to London, that he had been there to take charge. From the moment Tessa had said 'This time, it looks pretty bad', all animosity had vanished.

'He's in hospital?' Ryan had queried promptly, and fear had entered Meredith's heart when Tessa had replied gravely,

'He was in no condition to refuse to go, apparently.'

Vaguely Meredith was aware that she hadn't introduced the man she had married to her friend, but she rather gathered that Tessa had concluded who he was from the smart car which was parked by the kerb. Then Ryan was asking, 'Do you want anything from the cottage before we get off?' and, as her numbed heart overflowed with love for him that he, by the look of it, was prepared to take her back to London with all speed, she told him she would just go and collect her handbag.

Her anxiety grew greater as, whenever possible, Ryan kept his foot down, the quicker to get her to London. Mixed in with her worries for her uncle, though, was the anxiety of wondering how her great-aunt was coping.

'Do you want to go straight to the hospital or to see your aunt first?' Ryan enquired, just as if he knew what thoughts were going through her mind.

'Aunty will be at the hospital,' Meredith told him with conviction. And so it turned out to be.

Mrs Key was there too, and it was she who was outside the small side ward looking out for her. 'How are things?'

asked Meredith, hurrying towards her immediately she saw her.

'Not good,' Mrs Key replied, and added, 'Miss Simmons is with your uncle now.'

Thanking her for all she had done, Meredith went silently and quickly into the side ward where her tired and drawn-looking aunt was keeping vigil over her unconscious brother.

'I'm glad you're here,' she whispered as Meredith hugged her. 'Both of you,' she added as Meredith let her go and she observed that Ryan had come with her.

There was no change in Porter Simmons' condition over the next few hours, and as Meredith sat with her aunt at his bedside she was aware of Ryan there in the background, trying to make things easier for them.

It was he who brought them tea and sandwiches from somewhere, he who drove Mrs Key home when reluctantly she mentioned that she was baby-sitting that night, and Meredith was again grateful to him. It was Ryan too who, when a doctor came and checked on her uncle and declared that there was a slight improvement, drove them back to her old home.

Once there, she was staggered when she glanced at her watch and saw that it was nearly midnight. But, despite the fact that her aunt looked ready to drop, Meredith had to admire the way she remembered her manners as she told Ryan, 'You must have some supper.'

'I had something to eat at the hospital, thank you, Miss Simmons,' he told her gently, 'and...'

'And it's time you were in bed, Aunty,' Meredith took up. And, at her aunt's anxious look, 'The hospital will telephone us if—if there's any change in Uncle Porter's condition.'

'You and Ryan are staying the night?' Evelyn Simmons enquired.

'I—er...' Meredith began, feeling drained herself and for the moment stumped.

'Yes, of course,' Ryan replied, and Meredith was again grateful to him.

Though she was not quite sure how she felt when shortly afterwards, having locked up, he escorted both her and her aunt up the stairs. 'Goodnight, darling,' she bade her aunt gently as she kissed her cheek before coming away from her bedroom. Then Meredith, with Ryan right there beside her, went on to her own bedroom.

'Don't worry,' he said quietly when, with both of them inside her bedroom, she looked at him nonplussed.

Ryan could, she realised, have meant she was not to worry regarding her uncle. But, as common sense squeezed in through her tiredness, she realised that what he was saying was, Look, I couldn't do anything other in the circumstances than come along to your room. He was also saying, she realised, that as soon as her aunt was asleep he would go and sleep on the downstairs settee.

'I'm—not,' she said quietly, and, since she had left a suitcase of clothes in Derbyshire, she went to the chest of drawers and extracted a nightdress and a fresh cotton robe. Then, armed with both, she went to the small adjoining bathroom and washed and changed.

She felt only a little awkward when, nightdress- and robe-clad, she returned to the room. But Ryan, she felt, was the soul of tact when, turning from her to study a couple of out-of-date magazines on a small table, and keeping his voice down, he told her over his shoulder. 'Feel free to get into bed, Meredith, I'll be away shortly.'

She had hurriedly got into her bed, and had the bed-covers up to her chin when, with her eyes closed, she told him, 'Take your ease in the soft chair for a few minutes.' She heard the sound of him moving, then heard the creaking sound of the small bedroom chair as it took his weight. 'Goodnight,' she called.

'Goodnight, love,' he said softly, and Meredith had never loved him more. Because he was kind, and be-cause when, her emotions ragged over her uncle, she had needed someone to say a kind word, Ryan had called her 'love'.

Somehow, with Ryan still in the room, she fell asleep. How that came about when she was aware of him in the same room as her with every fibre of her being, she did not know. Nor did she know that she had fallen asleep until two hours later when she awakened in the darkened room to feel someone getting into bed with her!

'What...!' she started to shriek, but Ryan was quick to calm her agitation.

'Shh!' he breathed. 'It's all right,' he soothed, and in a low voice, 'I tried to go downstairs, but your aunt has her bedroom door open and called out to me,' he ex-plained. 'I was forced to come back and try to sleep in the chair. But that chair,' he said humorously, 'was made for a midget.'

Meredith owned to feeling slightly confused as she worked out that her aunt Evelyn must have left her bedroom door open with the intention of not missing hearing the phone should the hospital call. But, although every piece of intelligence was telling her she should tell Ryan in no uncertain terms to find somewhere else to sleep, somehow she could not do it. Aside from all the help he had been, the fact that he had sounded more amused than amorous, not to mention that he had perched himself right on the edge of the bed and could have been a mile away for all she could detect his presence, made it seem to her that to eject him was only being exceedingly petty.

'Goodnight,' she murmured and, turning her back on the other side of the bed, was soon drifting off to sleep again.

She slept only briefly this time, however, and awakened to find that at some moment in the intervening time, as she had turned over again to face her bed partner, so that bed partner had moved away from the edge of the bed to draw nearer to her.

Meredith was too disorientated to know how she felt when she began to appreciate that not only had they moved closer to each other, but she was now safely gathered up in Ryan's arms, and that her head was now— cradled on his shoulder!

Her body stiffened. It was all new to her, this lying in bed with a man. But, prompted a small voice, this man was her husband. This man was the man she loved. And suddenly all the stiffness went out of her body, and she rested against him.

She was still in his arms when she again awakened a couple of hours later. This time, though, she felt refreshed enough from sleep to make more clear evaluations and decisions.

Gently, in the early light of dawn, so as not to disturb him, she went to pull out of his arms with the purpose of leaving the bed and getting dressed. But she didn't get very far, because just as if he liked having her in his arms, Ryan's hold suddenly tightened—and Meredith knew that he too was awake.

'I'm g-getting up now,' she whispered falteringly as she raised her head and looked into the warm regard of his grey eyes.

'You don't sound very sure about that,' he murmured with a lazy smile, and suddenly, as he stretched out a naked arm to touch the arm that peeped out from her sleeveless nightdress, Meredith's heart began to pound.

'Oh—R-Ryan,' she said unsteadily, and was incapable of making or carrying out any decision when he moved to pull her tenderly closer to him.

'Relax, little love,' he said softly, and gently he laid his mouth over hers. And because she wanted his mouth over hers, Meredith relaxed as far as she was able and, with no thought in her head save for him, she stretched up to place her arms around his naked shoulders.

Again he gently kissed her, but as a flame surged into life in her at the touch of his nakedness, Meredith wanted more. Willingly her lips parted and, as his kisses became more ardent, she met his kisses with an ardency of her own.

She felt his hands warm through her nightdress at the back of her as he caressed her and traced tiny kisses down her throat. Then his warm hands were caressing to her front, and he had captured the throbbing, swollen globes of her breasts.

'Ryan!' she cried his name, and felt that fire burning in her for him begin to burn with an even greater intensity.

She clutched on to him, nevertheless, when, wanting to feel more of her silken skin, he went to remove her nightdress. 'No?' he queried, and she so loved him that, even when it must have been clear to him that she wanted him, it seemed he would have accepted a refusal from her.

'Yes,' she sighed, and she smiled as she whispered, 'I haven't—er—adjusted yet to being in bed with a—a man.'

'With your husband, my shy one,' he corrected her, and while his fingers busied themselves with her clothing, he tenderly kissed her.

A minute later he had moved her with him and they were both sitting in bed, without clothing. A minute later, he had captured her naked, silken, pink-tipped breasts in the most gentle of holds. 'Sweet love,' he breathed, 'sweet, untouched love,' and, with his naked chest tenderly pressing against the hardened peaks of her breasts, his lips over hers, he lay down with her. She felt his hands caressing her thighs and moaned in pleasure at what he was doing to her, and the wild emotion he was creating in her. She felt a moment's shyness when his touch became more intimate, but when she instinctively pulled back Ryan was there again to soothe her.

'Shh . . .' he gentled her. 'There's nothing to be afraid of.'

'I'm—n-not afraid,' she told him huskily, 'just . . .'

'I know,' he said understandingly, and kissed her and caressed her, until long minutes later, she felt tormented beyond enduring, and could think of nothing save that she wanted to be possessed by him.

'Oh, please!' she cried, in a fire of agony in her need for him, and she was lost to everything save him when Ryan called out her name—just as though he too was beside himself with desire—for her.

The next time Meredith awakened, a short while later, she was totally confused again. Earlier, there had been no confusion, just the clear knowledge that as Ryan had wanted her, so she had wanted him. But surely their making love with each other had to have more meaning than just the physical—or was she just being old-fashioned?

She realised that she was very probably being old-fashioned, though she doubted that she would feel any differently had she not been brought up in an old-fashioned household. In silence she gazed at the sleeping face of the man who had not so long ago been so infinitely gentle with her as he had led her step by tender step through to full womanhood. But as she gazed at him and her heart pounded again just from seeing him and remembering how it had been, Meredith knew she was never going to be able to think clearly until she had put some distance between them.

Being extremely careful not to wake him, for should he reach for her, she thought she might well again be lost, Meredith left the bed and, scooping up her robe as she went, tiptoed from the room.

Oh, how she loved him, she thought as she donned her robe outside on the landing, and was strongly pulled by a need to turn about swiftly and go and climb straight back into bed with him. But although it took some doing, she managed to resist that urge. She needed to think, not to give way to a natural instinct to feel his arms, strong and protective, about her.

She was not entirely certain what there was to think about as she went silently down the stairs and into the sitting-room. But, although she felt a mixture of clear-headedness and confusion, it was clear-headedness that won the day. For only a few minutes later she was able to realise that what lay at the bottom of her inner unrest was her knowledge that while she had given herself to Ryan in love, he had taken, not from love, but because he had to be the one to call the tune. It hurt that it was so, but there was no getting away from it. Ryan had wanted her biddable in his bed, and she—though she had determined that her days of being biddable were over—had given in totally, without a fight.

Her breath caught on a choky sound that she had been so unwary, so naïve, so—dammit—stupid as to listen to the dictates of her heart and her body instead of the intelligence of her head.

She had just finally decided that she was never going to be so weak as to allow Ryan Carlisle to make love to her again when, striking fear into her heart, the telephone rang. Instantly her thoughts were all for her great-uncle Porter. The clock on the mantel said twenty past six—who but the hospital would ring at this hour?

Conscious that if she let the phone ring much longer it would disturb her aunt, Meredith, after a moment of frozen immobility, went quickly to answer it. It was the hospital. Gently she was informed that her great-uncle had died.

'Thank you,' she said quietly, and replaced the receiver to turn and find that a fully-clothed Ryan had come silently into the room. 'Uncle Porter has died,' she told him woodenly, and when Ryan came forward and seemed as though he was about to take her in his arms, she snapped icily, 'Don't touch me!' Hearing a sound on the stairs, she ignored the sudden lift of his brow at this change in her from the clinging, passionate and vibrant woman she had been a short while ago, and went quickly past him and out through the hall to where her dressing-gowned aunt was nearing the bottom of the stairs.

'Was that the phone?' her aunt asked.

Meredith nodded, and, there being no way in which she could dress up the bad news, began, 'Aunty darling...'

An hour later, and because her aunt wished it, Ryan drove them to the hospital. And, despite Meredith's coolness towards him, he seemed prepared to take them wherever they wanted to go.

Indeed, it was he who the next day escorted them to the necessary authorities they had to visit in having Porter Simmons' death recorded, and his funeral arranged. But not once, in the days and nights that followed, did he enter again the bedroom he had shared with Meredith.

And Meredith would not have wanted it any other way. At least, that was what she told herself at the beginning. Had Ryan attempted again to take her in his arms in those days prior to her great-uncle's funeral, then she was sure the sharp feel of her hand on the side of his face was the minimum reception he would have got from her.

But he attempted no such thing and, conversely, on the day after her great-uncle was laid to rest, Meredith began to see why. All too plainly, having made love to her, having had her malleable under his will, he had now lost all interest.

That knowledge hurt, and Meredith was grateful that she had plenty to keep her occupied when her aunt asked her to go through her uncle's belongings on her behalf, and to dispose of them as she thought fit.

Meredith was grateful, too, to Lilian Peplow who, since Great-uncle Porter's death, was spending more time in their home than in her own home next door. Initially she had called to offer her condolences, but her visits had grown longer and longer, and having her there to befriend her aunt as the two talked over old memories of the years seemed to help her aunt over her grief at losing her younger brother and daily companion.

Meredith's own friend Tessa had telephoned on the Sunday of her uncle's death to enquire how he was. 'Oh, I'm so sorry,' she had said when Meredith had told her. 'How's your aunt taking it?'

'Much better than I would have supposed,' Meredith said.

'How about you?' Tessa had then asked.

'I'm fine,' she had replied, but, able to talk freely for once, with her aunt having a lie-down upstairs and Ryan having gone to fill up his car with petrol, Meredith was this time completely and utterly unable to confide in her friend when Tessa enquired,

'Is Ryan still with you?'

Meredith had been feeling decidedly cold towards Ryan that day. But even so, it just seemed beyond her to revile him to her friend. 'He's very kind,' she told her.

'I'm glad,' Tessa commented quietly, and, save to ask if Meredith thought she should come to the funeral, she had little else to add.

Meredith could see no particular reason why Tessa should attend. It was not as though she'd known her uncle well, and most likely, had Tessa wanted to come, she would not have asked.

It was odd, the way things had worked out, Meredith reflected, as upstairs in her uncle's room she parcelled up clothes to take to Oxfam. Her aunt had quite logically decided, when she and Ryan had arrived at the hospital on Saturday, that Ryan's business abroad was completed and that he had been up in Derbyshire collecting her to take her back to their apartment when Mrs Key had telephoned to say what had happened.

Being gullible must run in the family, Meredith thought sourly a moment later, for her aunt had entirely accepted that, while Ryan was occupied with looking after them and the arrangements, he was not doing any work. She saw it as perfectly feasible that he should return to his own home each evening to catch up on his day's work.

Well, he can jolly well stay at his home each evening! Meredith thought furiously, not sure if the stray tear that escaped was on account of the harrowing job she was tackling or because Ryan had so tenderly taken her to the heights, only to drop her down to the cold, desolate depths.

And he need not bother coming round to her aunt's home again either, she fumed, as she stiffened her backbone. But the next second she was very near to wilting, because it was obvious to anyone with even half an eye that, with her uncle buried and with no more arrangements being necessary, Ryan would not be coming round to her aunt's home again.

Hiding her hurt at his obvious belief that, having slept with her once, once was quite enough, thank you, Meredith immersed herself in the job she had to do. She was still upstairs sorting out her uncle's clothing that afternoon when the front door bell sounded.

For once her aunt was paying a visit to Lilian Peplow rather than the other way around, and, believing that her aunt had dropped the latch but forgotten to take her key, Meredith went swiftly down the stairs to let her in.

When she reached the door and opened it, though, she discovered that she was wrong on two counts. First, it was not her aunt on the other side of the door. Second, as her heartbeats quickened and she sternly wiped any sign of welcome from her face, Meredith saw that she was mistaken in her belief that Ryan would not be calling at her aunt's home again. For the tall man who stood cool grey-eyed and scrutinising her was none other than he!

Almost Meredith closed the door on him without a word. Her pride had wanted her to do just that, she owned. But Ryan had indeed been as kind as she had told Tessa he had been, and she would be beholden to no one.

Without a word, she turned and walked along the hall to the sitting-room. She was aware that he had crossed the threshold and that he had closed the door and was following, but only she was going to know about the nonsense that was going on inside her.

'My aunt's next door visiting Mrs Peplow,' she turned round to tell him coolly. 'I'll go and fetch her if you'd like to...'

'It isn't your aunt I've come to see,' he grated, his eyes narrowing. Quite clearly he did not care for her manner.

'Then you must have come to see me,' Meredith clipped icily. Though she felt forced to go on by the sheer weight of his authority when, without saying a word, he stared grim-faced at her. 'Although why,' she added aloofly, 'completely baffles me.'

'You don't think we have something to discuss?' he bore her aloof manner to enquire coolly, and Meredith felt quite ill inside. As clearly as if he had just said the word 'divorce', she knew quite well what he was there to discuss.

'I've—nothing to discuss with you,' she told him flatly, as she inwardly panicked and her pride fought a battle with her love for him. The love said that no matter what, she needed time to get adjusted to the thought of them being divorced. But her pride began to win, and it was again aloofly that she told him, 'I shall stay here with my aunt, so you...'

'Naturally you'll stay here with her un...' He broke off. Then as Meredith struggled up from the depths of her unhappiness that not only was he stating categorically that he did not want her living with him, he was amazing her by his sheer nerve, when he added, 'I used to think—before we married—that you had some small feeling for me. Has that all gone, Meredith? Or was it all pretence from the start?'

'My, what a short memory you have, Ryan!' she drawled, constantly amazed at her own reserves of strength—or maybe it was just pride making her determined not to let him see that she felt like a whipped puppy inside. 'You surely remember that I'd have pretended to like the devil himself in those days when I had the notion that I wanted to leave home? Although,' pride spurred her on, 'should I ever have been so idiotic as to have begun to care for you, then you can be darn sure that it wouldn't have survived my finding out—on our wedding day—what a cold, calculating rat you are!' Meredith had to break off to pause for breath, but, as Ryan took all she threw at him, her pride had returned in full measure when, just before she sailed from the room, she told him impersonally, 'And now, if you'll excuse me, I'll return to the job of sorting my uncle's belongings.'

Her legs might have been feeling dreadfully shaky, but she made it to the upstairs landing without faltering. She only realised that she was holding her breath and listening, though, when, after what seemed an age of silence from downstairs, she suddenly heard the front door open and close as Ryan let himself out.

A dry sob shook her as she sucked in fresh breath. What more proof did she need that he had come that

afternoon to ask her for a divorce? He had made no
attempt to stop her when she had walked away from
him—what more proof did she need that he did not care
a scrap about her?

CHAPTER SEVEN

IN THE month that followed, Meredith thought over countless times the way in which Ryan Carlisle had called on her the afternoon when her aunt had been next door. And each time she relived the way the conversation had gone, she came to the same conclusion—that Ryan had come to discuss their divorce.

Not that they had actually got around to talking about their divorce. She thought over again, as she had frequently, the panic that had beset her when she had been unable to face the finality of being divorced from him. Thank goodness her pride had come to her rescue in time, though, she mused, and she was again remembering how, mercilessly, in her opinion, Ryan had had the nerve to refer to the 'small feeling' which she had seemed to have for him.

She had since thanked her lucky stars that but for the confines of her strict upbringing she might well have been unable, in those days before their marriage, to refrain from showing him just how totally enraptured by him she was. Only by the skin of her teeth had she been able to show just how 'little' she did care that afternoon. All she hoped was that, if he ever got around to wondering why, if she had no particular feeling for him, she had given herself so willingly to him, he would think that she had given herself out of sheer propinquity, having found herself in the same bed with him, and from weakness when confronted with the expertise of his seduction.

Meredith got on with preparing the dinner that evening with Ryan still in her head. She did not know how to accept the thought of never seeing him again, but as she cleaned and sliced carrots it came to her that, not having seen him for a month, she had still pulled through.

She would pull through too, she determined fiercely. She had been fine before she had known him. Who was he anyway but...? Meredith set to work laying the table, aware that she was fooling no one but herself. She loved the rat, was in love with the arrogant swine; he was her world, and that was all there was to it.

It was over dinner with her aunt that Meredith was brought up short to realise that she was not fooling someone else on another front. She had previously explained that Ryan had suggested that, in these early days of her aunt losing her brother and companion of so many years, he thought it a good idea that she stay on at her old home for a while. But she was helping her aunt to some roast chicken that night when her aunt looked at her sharply, and told her, 'I think it's about time, Meredith, that you returned to your new home and began cooking dinner for your husband.'

'You don't want me to stay here any more?' Meredith took evasive action, having noted the no-nonsense look on Evelyn Simmons' face.

'It isn't that I don't want you here, child,' her aunt replied. 'Your presence in this house has brightened many a dark day. But,' she went on forthrightly, 'your place is with your husband.'

'I...' Meredith began, hesitated, and because she knew she could not go on avoiding this issue for ever, 'Actually, Aunty,' she got started again, 'Ryan and I—well, we're— er—not getting on too well at the moment.'

'How can you be getting on?' Evelyn Simmons questioned. 'You never see each other!'

'That's just it,' Meredith said quickly. 'We've decided on a—a trial separation.' The words, the painful words, were out. But as she looked at her aunt expecting to have to dash for the smelling salts, Evelyn Simmons surprised her by being more hardy than that. More hardy—and entirely disbelieving.

'Tosh!' she exclaimed. 'The two of you haven't had time to get beyond the honeymoon stage yet!'

'I made a mistake,' Meredith tried to tell her.

'Bunkum!' Her aunt refused to listen. And, heedless of what Meredith was trying to get across to her, she said bracingly, 'You're just not the sort to fall in and out of love every five minutes—you're too like your dear mother for that.' Having seen Meredith on her wedding day, and witnessed the stars shining in her eyes at the thought of being Ryan Carlisle's wife, she knew full well that her great-niece was heart and soul in love with him. 'Besides, Ryan is such a wonderful man, how could you fall out of love with him?' she asked, and, having never been married herself, she told her that the first year of marriage was always difficult, and spent the rest of that meal singing Ryan Carlisle's praises.

Wondering what her aunt would think of him were she to tell her that he had only married her to get his hands on the Burgess Electrical shares, and how—as simple as you like—she had fallen for it, Meredith left the table feeling mentally bruised and battered. Though no matter how mentally exhausted she felt from her aunt trying to get through to her that her husband was one in a million, it was utterly beyond her to be that disloyal to the man she loved.

They were in the sitting-room watching a programme on TV which was doing nothing to lift her from the unhappy reverie she had fallen into when suddenly the phone rang and, going over to answer it, she heard the pleasant voice of her friend Tessa.

'I'll go and make a cup of tea,' her aunt said, on hearing Meredith greet her friend by name.

'Sorry,' said Meredith when her aunt had trundled off, 'I missed what you were saying.'

'I was only asking how you were.'

'Fine,' Meredith replied.

'You don't sound it,' Tessa promptly came back, and caused Meredith to apologise again.

'I've just tried telling Aunt Evelyn that Ryan and I are separated. Aunt...'

'Heavens!' Tessa exclaimed.

'Absolutely. I'm afraid it didn't go down too well. Aunty sort of thinks that Ryan's pretty special.'

'And you?' Tessa queried.

'As my aunt so rightly said while we were having dinner—I'm just not the type to fall in and out of love every five minutes,' Meredith confessed, but, suddenly ashamed of being so weak, she asked brightly, 'How are things with you? Any new commissions or any... Say, I never asked how that fund-raising affair in your village went! Did you make lots of lovely money for charity with your "Portrait While You Sit" stall?'

'I did, and it was terrific,' Tessa told her enthusiastically. 'Luckily it was a super sunny day. Actually,' she added after a moment's pause, 'I was thinking of trying my hand at sketching sitters as a business venture. Since I suspect that it's going to be a tough world to break into commercially, though, and since that drawing I did of you, having more time than at the fête, was one of my best, not to mention the fact that you have more to recommend you than most,' she threw in lightly, 'you might do me a bit of good if you showed my artistic ability around.'

Tessa had gone on in the same light, joking vein to state that that particular portrait would be a splendid advert for her when, laughingly, Meredith interrupted her to state, 'If I had that sketch I'd be only too willing to show it around, but . . .'

'You haven't got it?' Tessa queried, but soon realised where the sketched portrait had disappeared to. 'Ah!' she said, and a second later. 'It's happened before; it must have happened again.'

'What . . .?' Meredith began.

'I must have left it on the kitchen dresser,' Tessa started to explain. 'The last time I did that—though that time it was a note for the coalman—I opened the sitting-room door a bit too quickly, and the draught wafted it off the dresser and underneath.' Meredith, remembering the heavy kitchen dresser, was mentally ahead of her friend when she said, 'Well, it'll have to stay there for a while; that dresser's so heavy, it only gets moved when I decorate. Come to think of it,' she added, 'it's never been moved.'

Feeling much happier than she had been feeling, Meredith was grateful to Tessa that she seemed set on cheering her up, and she briefly forgot her hurt about Ryan as they chatted on some more. Then suddenly she wondered how her friend's brother was faring now that he had a new girlfriend. 'How's Aldo?' she enquired.

'Don't ask!' Tessa sighed. 'His new girlfriend's chucked him, and he's fed up again.'

'Oh, dear!' Meredith sympathised.

'You can say that again,' Tessa murmured, and changed the subject to invite her to return to Little Haversham whenever she could. Shortly afterwards they said cheerio to each other, and Meredith went and shared a pot of tea with her aunt.

Meredith was out shopping the next afternoon when, with no salve seeming capable of healing her wounded heart, she paused to give thought to Aldo Wallace. He had appeared devastated when Caroline had walked out on him, and yet in no time he had taken up with someone else. True, by the sound of it that second relationship had barely got off the ground before his new girlfriend had thrown him over, but had he found some heart's ease during the brief period of dating someone else?

She returned home with her shopping and supposed that, to have considered how Aldo coped when his love-life went sour on him, she must have been seeking to find some way, some sort of an anodyne, to lessen her own pain. The way for her, however, she realised without having to think about it, did not lie through a new man-friend. Apart from the fact that she never went anywhere to meet someone new, the whole idea of dating anyone but Ryan was repugnant to her.

A smile curved her mouth as she let herself back into the house, however. She could just imagine what her aunt would have to say if she, a married woman, had any gentleman visitor come to the door for her other than the man she was married to.

'I'm back, Aunty!' she called as she went along the hall into the kitchen to unload her purchases.

'I'll put the kettle on.' Her aunt joined her in the kitchen. 'I've just had tea with Lilian, so I won't have a cup myself,' she said, but there was something in her voice which Meredith's sensitivity picked up as indicating that her aunt was worried about something.

'What's wrong, dear?' She halted in the middle of putting a bag of sultanas away, and turned to take in her elderly relative's disturbed expression.

'Nothing's wrong, exactly,' her aunt replied and, deciding to take a seat, she waited until her great-niece had decided that the stowing away of groceries could wait and had also taken a seat at the kitchen table; then she said, 'Harold came to see his mother on Saturday and, according to Lilian, he was quite sharp with her when she remarked how she'd been cleaning windows the day before. Anyhow, one thing led to another, and it ended up with Lilian saying that she wouldn't mind moving to a house that had fewer windows.'

'Mrs Peplow's thinking of moving?' Meredith enquired slowly, able to see immediately why her aunt was so disturbed. Mrs Peplow and her aunt had lived next door to each other for years. Mrs Peplow was part and parcel of next door, and Meredith could well understand her aunt's disquiet should her friend of so many decades think of moving.

'It hasn't got as far as that, but I'm sure it won't be long before the idea really takes root,' Evelyn Simmons said anxiously. 'Harold's already told her he isn't the least interested in inheriting the house. He's all for her selling up and buying something smaller and more manageable. According to him, she'd have the money over from the sale and would be much better off financially than she is now.'

By the sound of it, Harold was really putting the pressure on for his mother to sell up. But, because her aunt seemed so worried, Meredith tried the best she could to calm her fears. 'Perhaps when she's thought about it seriously she'll decide not to move,' she said gently. 'They're all large properties in this neighbourhood, anyway,' she inadvertently added fuel to the fire, 'so Mrs Peplow won't...'

'That's the whole worry of it,' her aunt butted in agitatedly. 'If Lilian wants to buy something smaller, she'll have to move out of the area and—and I'll probably never see her again. Oh, Meredith,' she said fretfully, 'I just don't know what I shall do if Lilian moves away!'

Meredith could have kicked herself for what she had said, and quickly she left her chair and went to put an arm about her great-aunt's shoulders. 'I'll still be here, darling,' she tried to make her feel better. 'And we can always take a taxi and go to see...' But her aunt had a very different viewpoint.

'You won't be here!' she interrupted her. 'Any day now you'll be returning to your husband—as you should have done before now. I don't know how you've managed to stay away from your married home for this long,' she went on, her tone growing disapproving, and Meredith realised that she might have got her aunt off the worry of what she was going to do if her friend and neighbour sold up, but only at the expense of her severest lecture so far on her duty to her husband, and her husband's home.

When Meredith finally got away from hearing her aunt's firmly expressed opinion on the sanctity of marriage, she escaped up to her room, and wondered why she should feel the loyalty she did to Ryan. He did not deserve that she should hold back from telling her aunt what a cold and calculating toad he was, and that he had not meant a word of the vow 'to love and to cherish' that he had made in that church. And yet she had taken a good half-hour of her aunt persistently, if quietly, hammering away, her main theme being that it would please her better if she went and kept her 'till death us do part' vow, rather than stay with her.

She braved going down the stairs again in the early evening when she realised that she couldn't leave it any later to make a start on the dinner. She knew in her heart that she was welcome in her old home, but that it was just that it went against everything her aunt believed in that she and her husband should live apart.

In the kitchen Meredith busied herself making a winter salad, which her aunt especially enjoyed, while she silently mused that she did not see how she could possibly leave her aunt anyway—particularly if Mrs Peplow was likely to be moving.

Tessa had invited her back to Little Haversham, she ruminated, but there was no way she could go and stay— not for more than a night or two, anyway—and leave her seventy-nine-year-old aunt on her own.

So how in creation was she supposed to leave the dear soul to go and live with that chauvinistic swine she had married? How, for that matter, could she tell her aunt that he would probably have bars and bolts fitted to his door against her, should she so much as hint that she might be taking up permanent residence in his abode?

Beating eggs for cheese omelettes, another of her aunt's favourites, Meredith could see no way out of any of her difficulties. It seemed to her, in a moment of dark despair, that life was being a bit of a pill just at present.

Which was perhaps why, when Aldo Wallace rang her most unexpectedly later that evening, Meredith, maybe seeking some sort of relief, acted in a way which she would not have considered earlier.

Dinner had passed with her aunt being pleasant but for the most part preoccupied. But, since Meredith was fairly certain that what occupied her aunt's thoughts must be either or both of the subjects which they had last discussed, she did not think that to invite a renewal of the discussion would be in anyone's interests. Nothing her aunt said was going to change the fact that she was living apart from her husband, nor would it do either of them any good. Nor, as far as she could see, would it help for her to suggest that Mrs Peplow might not sell up and leave when her aunt, having spoken with Lilian Peplow more recently than she had, better knew what her friend was more likely to do.

'I'll bring the coffee into the sitting-room if you like, Aunty,' she told her when they had finished the washing up from dinner.

No sooner had Meredith arrived in the sitting-room with a tray of coffee, though, than the phone rang. 'It's for you,' her aunt advised, having answered the instrument while Meredith set the tray down.

Instantly Meredith's heart was all of a flutter. Had it been Tessa on the other end of the phone, Tessa would have delayed her aunt to have had a few words with her. Meredith's heart settled to a dull beat, however, when she realised that the same could be said of Ryan. Somehow, and despite the many faults which she was prepared to attribute to him, she could not see him being so impolite as to ask to speak to her without first passing the time of day with her aunt.

Wondering why the heck she should think that Ryan might ring anyway, Meredith took the phone from her and said, 'Hello,' down the mouthpiece.

'Hello to you, Meredith, it's Aldo,' a male voice that was nowhere near as attractive as her husband's replied.

Since Aldo had never phoned her before and as far as she knew did not know the Simmons surname to look her up in the book, Meredith had to gather her scattered senses to latch on to who he was.

'How are you, Aldo?' she enquired, suddenly aware that, where before her aunt had afforded her every privacy, she was not making any excuse to do something in the kitchen in this instance of her being telephoned by some male who clearly was not Ryan Carlisle.

'About the same as you, by all accounts,' Aldo answered, and, getting to the point of his call, 'Tessa tells me your husband is away on business for some while, and that you need cheering up.'

'I don't!' Meredith denied, as she wondered what had prompted Tessa to tell him anything of the sort.

'Well, I do!' he said. 'Which is why, at enormous expense, I've managed to get hold of a couple of tickets for a musical which I know you're just going to love.'

'You're asking me to go with you?' she enquired, and caught her aunt's quick look at her.

'I certainly haven't rung to ask your aunt,' he replied, and asked, 'Are you going to come with me, Meredith, or have I thrown my money down the drain?'

'When are the tickets for?' she enquired, wondering why she was enquiring anything of the sort, because there was not one single item pencilled in on her social calendar and nobody used 'I'm washing my hair' as an excuse these days, did they?

'Next Tuesday,' he told her, adding, 'It was the earliest date I could get. Tessa's given me your address,' he went on, and as if it was all settled, 'I'll call for you in plenty of time.'

'Thank you,' Meredith murmured, and it seemed that the whole thing *was* settled, for Aldo rang off.

Slowly she returned the phone to its rest and realised that, for all she had laughed quite a bit during her last telephone conversation with Tessa, she had not for a minute fooled her friend about how down she truly felt. She suspected too that Tessa, by telling her brother what she had about her husband being away on business, was leaving it up to her to tell Aldo as much or as little as she wanted.

'Was that "Aldo" Tessa's brother?' her aunt, unable to contain her curiosity, broke in through Meredith's thoughts.

'Er—yes,' she owned, and, sensing trouble before she began, 'He's invited me to the theatre next Tuesday.'

'You're not going, of course.'

'I am, actually,' Meredith replied quietly.

'Do you think that's wise, dear?' Evelyn Simmons enquired as though trying really hard to get to grips with the thinking of the younger generation. 'I don't think your husband would take very kindly to you having gentlemen friends, do you?'

To Meredith's way of thinking, her husband would not give a tuppenny damn how many 'gentlemen friends' she had, but, out of respect for her great-aunt's years, she refrained from saying as much, but confessed to the truth of it as she answered, 'I don't consider Aldo Wallace as a man-friend, Aunty, but more the brother of a friend. It sort of puts him in a different category,' she added, and realised, when she later climbed into bed, that as far as she was concerned that just about summed up how she felt about Aldo. She had earlier that day felt the idea of dating any man but Ryan to be totally repugnant. But she felt no such repugnance about going to the theatre with Aldo, quite simply because, with him being her good friend's brother, she just did not look on him as a date.

The weekend had to be got through before Tuesday, though, and Meredith spent most of it telling herself—as though telling would make it fact—that she was really going to enjoy going to the theatre.

It turned out to be a wet weekend, with the rain hitting the window-panes non-stop, so any idea she might have had to go a short walk with her aunt to maybe take her mind off her worries about Lilian Peplow's moving did not materialise.

It was still raining on Monday, and Meredith had proof that her aunt was indeed worrying when shortly after lunch she announced that she had a headache and was going upstairs to lie down for a while.

'I'll mix you a couple of aspirins, shall I, Aunty?' Meredith enquired.

'I'll manage without, I think, Meredith dear,' her aunt, a staunch anti-pill taker, replied. 'Probably the weather has as much to do with it as anything.'

Meredith was not duped for a second. But she watched as her aunt slowly climbed the stairs and wished there was something she could do which would ease her worries. If Lilian Peplow did decide to leave, though, Meredith could not see that there was anything that she, or anybody else could do about it.

Wondering if it was too soon to have cheese omelettes and winter salad again, she went to the kitchen and was just thinking along the lines of having something special for dinner when the front door bell sounded.

As she went to answer it, her mind was more on what would please her aunt's palate than on who might be on the other side of the door. But when she pulled the door open, every thought of the meal that evening vanished.

'Good afternoon, Meredith,' said the tall, grey-eyed man pleasantly.

A smile began somewhere deep inside her. But even as that smile rushed upwards and her heart leapt with joy to see the man she felt starved for the sight of, her pride roared into action. Who was she, what was she, that after the way he had behaved she should greet him with open arms?

Her smile never made it, and when she spoke, her voice was far from welcoming when, not waiting for him to state why he was there, and in contrast to his pleasant manner, she coldly and abruptly told him, 'My aunt's lying down and doesn't wish to be disturbed.'

'I haven't called to see Miss Simmons,' Ryan clipped, her antagonistic tone clearly not going down very well. 'I...'

'If you've come to see me,' Meredith cut through whatever it was he had been about to say, 'then you've had a wasted journey. I want neither to see you nor to talk to you,' she told him spiritedly, and saw from the aggressive and sudden jut of his jaw that he had not reckoned on her having any spirit when he had married her.

'Damn your...' he began, but as if determined not to start a blazing row on her doorstep—for she was not inviting him in—he checked.

Looking into his suddenly cold grey eyes, Meredith wanted them warm for her. Even as she fired, 'And damn yours too!' she desperately wanted to feel his arms about her. Even as they stared hostilely at each other, she yearned quite hopelessly to rest her head against his chest, and felt, in an insane moment of weakness, that she would have given anything to have been able to do just that. But the days of her reacting instinctively to her feelings were long gone, and that weak moment dis-

solved as common sense reminded her how untrust-
worthy her instincts had been in the past.

But Ryan, having checked what he had been about to
say, seemed to have found some control. 'Good afternoon, Meredith,' he began again. 'I've called to...'

'Waste my time!' she chopped him off—it was either
that or be swamped by his charm. 'Well, I don't need
you, Ryan Carlisle, now or ever!' she blazed. 'So you
can...'

She did not get any further. Twice Ryan had tried to
be nice to her. She rather thought that was a record. He
was not, he made it abundantly plain, going to try a
third time. 'You may be able to totally ignore your responsibilities,' he sliced sharply through what she was
saying, 'but I'll not ignore mine. I've...'

'You look on me as a responsibility?' she flared
aggressively.

Angrily Ryan glowered at her. 'Hell's teeth!' he
snarled. 'You're so...' He broke off, and seemed to be
searching all the while to keep a hold on his temper,
which she seemed to be having the uncanniest knack of
provoking. 'Dammit, Meredith,' he said, a tough note
still in his voice, although his tone was quieter, 'you're
innocent enough not to know your way around the big
world. Y...'

'No, I'm not!' she contradicted him tartly, feeling that
she was fighting for survival—she had been weak before,
and look where it had got her. 'Thanks to you,' she went
on acidly, 'innocent is exactly what I'm not!' For her
sins, she discovered that she had triggered Ryan's anger
again, though she hardly thought that the accusatory
nature of what she had said bothered him one whit.

But, 'Saints preserve us,' he roared, 'you reckon one
night in bed with a man makes you less innocent—less

worldy-wise—than you were? You may have lost your virginity, but . . .'

'That's all I am losing!' Meredith yelled, her brilliantly blue eyes flashing as she glared into taken-aback-looking grey eyes, her new-found temper spiralling. How could he refer to what had been so beautiful in her memory in such a tough and uncaring way? 'If you have any respect for me whatsoever after—after that episode,' she blazed on, 'then you'll do me the courtesy of not calling here again!'

Meredith knew as those words left her that she was very close to hot, scalding and shaming tears. There was only one thing she could do. Without another word, she closed the door on him.

CHAPTER EIGHT

THERE was a secretive kind of look in her aunt's expression as they sat at the breakfast table together the following morning, or so Meredith thought. On this occasion, however, she did not enquire into her aunt's little secrets.

Having just spent one of the worst nights of her life, the restlessness she had experienced before was back again, and Meredith felt stifled and in need of going somewhere. Though because she had no intention of leaving her elderly relative alone for any great length of time, the best she could come up with to satisfy this calling to be off somewhere was to go clothes-shopping.

'I think I'll go and look for something a bit different to wear to the theatre tonight,' she remarked as she cut her toast in two.

'You do that, dear,' Evelyn Simmons replied, to Meredith's pleased surprise appearing to have accepted the truth of her telling her that she considered her theatre escort more the brother of her friend than in the 'man-friend' class.

'I might be some time,' she thought to mention, having no interest whatsoever in buying anything new, but feeling that if she stayed out until gone midnight she would still not have got rid of the restlessness within her.

'That's quite all right, Meredith, dear,' her aunt smiled. 'Have lunch out if you feel like it. Mrs Key will be here at nine, but in any case I want to go round and have a chat with Lilian later—it could,' she added mysteriously, 'take me some time too.'

Meredith left the house shortly after the daily help had arrived, and spent a morning going over and over again the many things that had kept her awake last night.

By her standards, that had been quite some slanging match between her and Ryan on her doorstep yesterday. She thanked goodness that their nearest neighbour, apart from Mrs Peplow who was a trifle deaf, lived quite some way down the avenue.

Not that Ryan Carlisle had seemed to bother who overheard them, she mused, as she went into one shop and browsed through a few clothes rails and came out again. Cheeky swine, him and his 'You may be able to totally ignore your responsibilities, but I'll not ignore mine'! She would not be his responsibility, she would not!

'I'm just browsing,' she smiled at an assistant who came forward as she entered the next shop, but her mind was again engaged elsewhere as she flipped through dresses on the various rails.

Nor, she fumed, as without buying anything she left that shop and went to have a cup of coffee, would she accept that she had any responsibility to him.

It had taken her an age when she had tried to work out what his 'You may be able to totally ignore your responsibilities' had meant. What responsibility had *she* ignored, for goodness' sake! But, since she did not think she had been remiss in connection with any responsibility towards her family, the only answer that would fit seemed to be that Ryan had been referring to the responsibility of being his wife!

Feeling emotionally drained, Meredith continued on her round of the shops and owned that she didn't think

she could take much more. She had told Ryan that if he
had any respect for her he would not call at her home
again, but he was a law unto himself. Regardless that
he evidently felt some sort of responsibility for her, he
would do exactly as he pleased anyhow.

She had her lunch out as her aunt had suggested, but
it was only as she made her way home that it came to
her what she must do. She had been burying her head
in the sand about the possibility of her and Ryan getting
divorced, she realised. She had panicked, she admitted,
when he had called that time before with 'something to
discuss'—not that he now seemed in any particular hurry,
or surely he'd have taken a different line when he had
called yesterday? But she supposed she must have ma-
tured considerably over these past weeks, for divorce
suddenly seemed to her to be the only clear-cut answer.

Rounding the corner into the avenue where she lived,
she decided that nor would she try to hide from her aunt
what she was doing. As soon as she arrived home she
would come out into the open and tell her—gently, of
course—everything that was happening. Aunt Evelyn was
going to have to accept that not all marriages were made
in heaven and that hers, for one, was giving her emotional hell.

Temporarily, though, all thoughts of a divorce and
how she would set about telling her aunt left Meredith
when, on entering the house, she saw a business-suited
man she had never seen before in conversation with her
aunt. She had noticed a car parked outside, but it had
seemed to be more outside Mrs Peplow's house, and she
had thought Mrs Peplow was the one with the visitor.

'Ah, there you are, Meredith!' Her great-aunt broke
off from what she was saying when she saw her, but,
too involved apparently to refer to the absence of any

dress-shop carrier, she said, 'This is Mr Bartram from Tranter's, the estate agents. He's just doing a little measuring.' And while Meredith was trying not to blink as she wondered what in the name of goodness her aunt was up to, her aunt was giving her something else to think about when she told Mr Bartram proudly, 'This is my grand-niece, Mrs Ryan Carlisle.'

'How do you do, Mrs Carlisle,' Mr Bartram said, as he stepped forward to shake her hand. But by the time Meredith had recovered from the delicious thrill of being called Mrs Carlisle, both her aunt and Mr Bartram were in another room.

Half an hour later Mr Bartram, having been offered a cup of tea by Evelyn Simmons but having politely declined, was being shown out by her. Meredith still had no clue to what was going on, but, since it was her view that it would not hurt her aunt to sit down for a short while, she made a tray of tea and carried it into the sitting-room. Thirty seconds later, a rather amazed Evelyn Simmons joined her.

'I can't get over it,' she said, if shaken, then looking shaken in a pleased way.

'Can't get over what, darling?' asked Meredith, keeping a watchful eye on her aunt as she seated herself in her usual chair.

'You remember how Porter was always moaning about the value of our money going down and down?'

'I remember,' Meredith confirmed quickly.

'Well, what I'm sure he didn't know, or he'd have said, was that the value of our property has gone up and up! Why,' said Aunt Evelyn as she started to recover, 'my father paid only hundreds for this house, but according to Mr Bartram it's now worth thousands and thousands!'

'You've—had the house valued?' Meredith queried, and, following that with what seemed to her to be a logical question considering the recent demise of the only Simmons male, 'You need to have a value for probate or something to do with Uncle Porter's will?' she asked.

'Oh, there's no need for that,' Evelyn Simmons said contentedly. 'The house didn't belong to Porter, or to Ogden either. It was always mine.' And, while Meredith took in what she was hearing, now, for the first time, her aunt explained briefly, 'My father, your great-grandfather, was one of the old school. He didn't believe in women going out to work, so when it didn't look as though I was going to get married he left the house to me.'

'I didn't know that!' Meredith exclaimed.

'It was a sore point with both Ogden and Porter, so it made for peace all round if nothing was said on the subject,' Evelyn smiled. 'Anyhow, I always knew that Father intended there should be a home here for both the boys should they want one, and that his willing the house to me was just his way of seeing to it that I had some security. When Ogden's wife died and he was left with a ten-year-old daughter, your mother, it seemed only right that Ogden should move back here.'

'So you could help bring my mother up,' Meredith said gently.

'Oh, I don't know about that. Ogden had very strict ideas about your mother's upbringing and employed a governess for her. Anyhow,' Evelyn Simmons seemed to give herself a mental shake, 'who'd have thought that this house would be worth such a vast sum? I must ring Lilian to see how she got on!'

'Mrs Peplow...' Meredith began, feeling a shade puzzled.

'Of course, I didn't tell you, did I?' her aunt smiled, and went on to reveal what the secretive look she had worn at breakfast had been about. 'You know that, with it being such a dreadful day yesterday, Lilian telephoned instead of coming round?'

'She rang just before lunch as I was on my way to the kitchen,' Meredith recalled.

'That's right. Well,' her great-aunt took a breath, 'what she rang to tell me was that Harold had made her see sense and she was selling up, and that Harold had fixed up for the man from Tranter's to come round and value her property today.'

'Mr Bartram has valued Mrs Peplow's property as well as yours today?' Meredith queried, recalling how worried her aunt had seemed after lunch yesterday.

'Yes,' Evelyn nodded. 'Of course I hadn't arranged then for Mr Bartram to come here too. But after Lilian told me what she did, and also how, while she didn't mind leaving her draughty old house, she was going to mind like billy-o not having me next door, I got to thinking.'

'You thought—that you might sell up too?' Meredith brought out that which seemed naturally to jell.

'I did,' her aunt agreed. 'As soon as I thought respectable this morning, I went round to see Lilian to enquire how she'd feel if I sold up too and we tried to buy new—and smaller of course—properties near to each other.'

'Mrs Peplow liked the idea?' Meredith queried, having thought that there was nothing new she could learn about her aunt, but discovering that, in certain circumstances, she was a speedy mover.

'She was extremely relieved at my suggestion,' Evelyn Simmons beamed. 'And in fact, she had a suggestion of

her own to make: that instead of buying two small properties next door to each other, we might buy one large
flat between us. We might even move to the coast,' she
announced, and, with a smile beaming from her again,
beamed, 'Isn't it exciting? I can see absolutely nothing
wrong with the idea. What with Porter gone and you
married and shortly returning to your husband, this
house is far, far too big for one.'

'It—certainly is exciting,' Meredith nodded, but the
last part of what her aunt had said had triggered off the
thought that, for all she had sounded totally genuine,
was this all some gigantic ruse of her aunt's to get her
to 'return' to Ryan? Suddenly Meredith found that she
was doing a rethink on her decision to bring her plans
to end her marriage out into the open. And she kept
them to herself still when she enquired tentatively,
'Would you still be thinking of moving if—er—Ryan and
I were to—er—divorce?'

The change in her aunt's expression was dramatic, as
she replied frostily, 'Yes, I should. Though it's to be
hoped, Meredith that you would never shame the family
by going through any divorce court!'

Meredith was upstairs getting ready to go to the theatre
that night when she ceased wondering at her weakness
in not telling her aunt her intention of ending her marriage. It was not so much weakness, she realised as she
stepped into a stylish, silky-look dress of deep blue, but
concern that her aunt had had a surfeit of excitement
for the time being.

Going downstairs to wait for Aldo, Meredith had even
begun to wonder if she and Ryan could be divorced
without her aunt ever knowing. Aunt Evelyn had spoken
of moving to the coast. Providing no newspaper re-
porter discovered the fact that Ryan Carlisle of Carlisle

Electronics was now divorced—and the signs looked good, for not one of them had picked up the information that he had married—Meredith thought that for her aunt's peace of mind she might be tempted to try it.

At all events, she realised that, with the house being sold, she would soon have to start looking for somewhere else to live. She had just seen that her one-time stated intention to find herself a flat—and a job—was coming nearer all the time when Aldo Wallace arrived to take her to the theatre. Meredith had just introduced the smartly attired man to Evelyn Simmons, and they were about to get on their way, when her aunt made her blink by asking, 'What shall I tell your husband if he rings while you're out?'

'Oh—just tell him where I am,' Meredith smiled at her as it all at once penetrated that what her suddenly wily aunt was about was to make certain that Aldo Wallace was aware—just in case he was not already— that his companion for the evening was a married woman.

It had crossed Meredith's thoughts to consider that Aldo might ask a question or two on the way to the theatre about her husband's absence. But, save for the remark, 'Life's a bind when the one you love isn't around,' which merely showed fellow feeling, the journey to the theatre consisted mainly of Aldo telling her how he was trying to get back with Caroline.

Respite from a repetition of what she had heard pretty well non-stop before came when they entered the theatre. 'You've managed to get some good seats,' she smiled to him as they were shown to their places in the stalls, and then, for the few minutes that were left before the curtain went up, she studied the programme which he had handed her.

At least, that had been her intention when she had opened up the programme. But suddenly, and without knowing at all why—for there was no reason for it—her eyes were drawn, as if compelled, upwards and over to the left. And that was when Meredith, her world falling apart for the second time, knew that Ryan Carlisle would not be ringing her home that night—not unless he did it in the theatre interval, anyhow. Though she could not see him leaving his stunning-looking companion on any such whim!

Somehow—foolishly, she admitted, since Ryan was every bit a virile male—she just had not thought of him dating other women. But as she stared at the one box whose occupants stood out from all the rest in the theatre, while she noted that there were four people in the box, the other two faded into insignificance. Only her husband and the person nearest to him—in age as well as physically—stood out, and Meredith saw for herself that he did indeed date other women, his date for this evening in particular being a most attractive and elegantly turned-out dark-haired woman.

But, as her eyes had been drawn to that certain box, so in those first few seconds of her world being turned upside down she realised that, just as she had spotted Ryan and his companion, he had spotted her and Aldo.

But even though she felt as if she had just been struck the most crippling blow, her pride was not dimmed. When coldness, not to say antagonism, seemed to beam a straight icy line down from Ryan to her, and not so much as a smile or a wave of acknowledgement did he give, Meredith was swift to think: well, two could play at that game. 'I didn't know she was in it!' She took her eyes off him to smile at Aldo, exactly as if she had just noticed that some famous personality was listed in the programme.

She was never more glad that at that moment the theatre lights began to dim. As well as not being able to show Aldo the fictitious person she had been referring to in the programme, she welcomed the darkness in order to get herself together.

She did not enjoy the performance. Though, as she truthfully owned, she had very little idea of what was going on on stage. She was overwhelmingly conscious of Ryan through the whole of the first half, and she never quite knew how she kept her eyes from going repeatedly upwards and to the left.

'Let's join the scrum and get a drink,' Aldo suggested when the lights went up again at the start of the interval.

Without hesitation Meredith left her seat. It was one thing to sit in the dark knowing Ryan was there, but quite another to sit in full view of him and try to pretend she had never felt happier—not that he was likely to stare down at her again.

As she waited with Aldo for the people further along the row to move out into the aisle, though, she just could not resist another look up. Her heart sank further down to the depths when she saw that the box Ryan had been in was now empty, proving he had better things to do than to sit staring down at her.

Step by small step, with Aldo in front, they edged their way out of the row and up the gangway of the stalls with the rest of the crush going for refreshments. Aldo was still in front as she went through the stalls entrance along with the masses and, to avoid the stairs leading down from the circle, took a sharp right turn.

Meredith had just stepped into an area at the bottom of the stairs, however, when suddenly a pair of strong masculine hands shot out and in one movement had plucked her into the only space where no one seemed to want to go.

'Do you mind?' she snapped, the fire in her angry words hiding the turmoil that was going on inside her from being this close with her tall, superbly suited and most definitely appealing husband.

To her undying gratitude Ryan let go the tight grip he had on both her arms, but his manner was as tough as his look as he demanded furiously, 'What the hell sort of game do you think you're playing?'

The jackal! The nerve of him! Incensed by his accusing tone, she denied her fast-beating heart. 'As sure as hell not the same extra-marital game you're playing— you can be certain of that!' Meredith, with veritable sparks spitting from her bright blue eyes, hurled at him. She saw his brow shoot up, though whether because she had just accused him of having an adulterous relationship outside of his marriage or because he had heard jealousy in her voice she was not stopping to find out. But before she left, and to make fully certain he knew he must be mistaken over any idea that she might be jealous, Meredith let go with an angry, 'I want a divorce,' and, noting that the crowd making for the bar had thinned out, she turned swiftly round and went as quickly as she could to catch up with Aldo.

The rest of the musical passed in a haze as far as she was concerned, and she was glad when it was time for Aldo to take her home.

'Thanks for a terrific evening,' she told him when, having apologised for not inviting him in on account of her aunt being asleep, she said her goodbyes to him.

'It was good, wasn't it,' he said, and with the words, 'We must do it again if your husband's going to be away for any length of time,' he watched her let herself into her home.

'Still up?' she enquired of her aunt, who was almost always in bed by ten.

'Was it a good play?' Evelyn Simmons countered.

'I'll lock up,' said Meredith, and despite the gremlins that were gnawing away at her she had to grin. Her aunt knew full well that the *play* had been a *musical*. 'I'm going to miss you,' she told her affectionately when the two of them went up the stairs.

'I don't expect, with that fast car of your husband's, I'll be very far away,' her aunt got one in before she turned into her room.

'I don't expect you will,' Meredith agreed, seeing no sense in upsetting her by telling her that she had, only a few hours ago, told her fast-car-owning husband that she wanted a divorce.

Having spent half the night lying awake being torn apart by a new and very dreadful emotion called jealousy, Meredith finally fell into an exhausted sleep in the early hours of Wednesday morning. The consequence was that she overslept and, even though she rushed around madly, she still didn't make the breakfast table for the usual time.

'Good morning, Aunty. Sorry I'm late—I overslept,' she said as she hurried into the breakfast room.

'I'll forgive you,' her aunt smiled. 'Although I should like to make an early start.'

'On what, darling?' Meredith enquired, blaming Ryan Carlisle for the fact that, though she was showered and dressed and had made it downstairs, her brain did not appear to have woken up yet.

'Why, on the packing, dear!' Evelyn Simmons exclaimed.

'Packing?'

'It won't do itself,' her aunt replied. 'And I've a col-lection of eighty years of living in this house to sort through.'

'Oh, I see,' Meredith said, and even though the estate agent's board had not been put up in the garden yet, much less a buyer having been found for the house, she enquired, 'Where would you like to start?'

'Attic or basement?' Evelyn Simmons seemed undecided.

'Attic,' Meredith opted, deciding that, since the basement was not the warmest place, she had better tackle that section of the house herself.

She was glad to be busy that day. She needed to be busy that day. But, as busy as she was, running up and downstairs with plastic bags full of waste which in due course she would have to coax the dustmen to take, she could not get Ryan nor his very attractive date of last evening from her mind.

And, in remembering his sophisticated female com-panion, Meredith's estimation of her own charms took a severe blow. How on earth, in those early days, those days before they had married, had she ever been so crass as to let herself believe he had fallen in love with her? With the evidence of the stylish women he went for etched in her brain, Meredith again died a thousand deaths to think that she had ever been such an idiot.

But having been so down, the only way then was up. It was around three that afternoon that, having per-suaded her aunt that it might be an idea if she went and had a little rest, she discovered that her aunt would only agree to rest if she broke off too.

'I could do with taking a bath and washing my hair,' Meredith told her, having pulled, prodded and pushed boxes and cases around prior to carrying them to her aunt to sort through.

Ryan was in her head the moment she left her aunt, as he had been off and on since she had opened her eyes that morning. But this time, instead of her feeling defeated, mutiny had set in. So all right, she might not have the sophistication of his female 'friend' of last night, but Ryan himself had once called her lovely, and had also commented to Monte Montgomery that she was beautiful.

Who the hell was Ryan Carlisle, anyway? Having hit rock-bottom, Meredith had no mind to stay there. The nerve of that man! she fumed again as she bathed and then shampooed her hair. Who was he to demand, in that accusing way he had, 'What the hell sort of game do you think you're playing?'? For, no matter how many times she looked at his accusing question, she could see it no other way: he was daring to take her to task for being at the theatre with some other man!

She fumed even more when later her aunt went around to next door to have a chat with Mrs Peplow, and she set about preparing dinner and thought again of his colossal effrontery. Her heart gave a crazy leap of excitement, just the same, when the ridiculous notion came fleetingly to her that for him to act in such a—'possessive' was the only word that fitted—possessive kind of way surely had to mean that he felt he had some rights over her?

It *was* ridiculous, and she tossed the notion away. Ryan had no rights, nor did he want any. She remembered then how he had claimed that it was up to him to provide for her, and she was confused again at the complex man he was, and again she was briefly defeated.

She rallied, however, to rail silently against him again. The fact that he should actually have dared to question her the way that he had at the theatre while, figuratively speaking, he'd had that stunning-looking woman on his arm made Meredith wish she had said far more than she had.

The trouble was that one always thought of something brilliant and cutting after the event. Though perhaps there had not been very much to add after her final, 'I want a divorce.'

Her aunt looked quite pleased with life when they sat down to dinner, and was full of the plans she and Lilian Peplow were making. Which in turn reminded Meredith that she should be doing something about her own plans.

That evening she and her aunt washed up together while Evelyn Simmons chatted away, and Meredith tried to keep her concentration on what she was saying while wishing she could find some of her aunt's enthusiasm for finding somewhere else to live.

Meredith was loading up the coffee tray prior to taking it into the sitting-room when they heard the phone ringing. 'I'll go,' Evelyn Simmons said, and was on the way to the sitting-room as she added, 'It might be Lilian with some more information.'

Smiling quietly to herself that the two near-octogenarians were acting just like a couple of school-girls, Meredith finished loading the tray and followed in the direction her aunt had gone.

No sooner had she entered the room, though, than she at once knew that it was not her aunt's friend on the telephone. For, 'It's for you,' her aunt told her, and, saying the pleasantest goodbye down the mouthpiece, which at once told Meredith that it was not Aldo Wallace on the other end, she held out the receiver to her.

Meredith's mouth went dry as she took the phone from her aunt. Which she instantly recognised was absolutely stupid, since her caller was most likely going to be Tessa anyway. Perhaps though it was that something, something which she could not quite put her finger on, in her aunt's pleased look that made her dry-throated and wary.

Finding her voice, she said, 'Hello.' Then she promptly went weak at the knees when the most superb voice to her in all the world answered. Though the way he answered swiftly made her stiffen, and at once stung her into feeling mutinous again.

'Since you clearly don't want me in your home, you'd better come here to my place!' he grated, apparently suddenly given to ordering her around.

'Why the h...' she immediately started to respond, but just in time she remembered that her aunt was still in the same room '...dickens,' she amended quickly, 'should I?'

'I refuse to discuss our divorce in the street, on your doorstep, or in the foyer of some theatre!' Ryan rapped back toughly. 'I'm going away tomorrow,' he added sharply, and was the bossiest she had known him as he commanded, 'Come now!' and bang, his phone went down.

For several seconds after the line went dead, Meredith stayed gripping on to the receiver. At first she could not take in the fact that, in answer to her request that he do the courtesy of not calling at her home again—and clearly having taken exception to having their domestic matters discussed in front of a theatre audience—Ryan had telephoned to order her to come to his place. Then she was totally stunned that in response to her demand for a divorce last night, he had rung to agree that he too wanted a divorce.

Knowing deep in the heart of her that she did not want a divorce, Meredith replaced the receiver and was suddenly beset by raging jealousy. So much for her thinking that Ryan was in no hurry about getting a divorce! Screaming jealousy twisted unmercifully at her insides as she realised just then why Ryan was so agreeable to a divorce—and for him to ring so promptly must mean that he was now impatient to get the divorce under way. His reason, of course, being none other than the woman he had been at the theatre with last night!

'Is something wrong, dear?'

Her aunt, her voice sounding concerned, quickly brought Meredith to an awareness that she was not alone. 'No, no, nothing at all,' she answered as blithely as she could. But because she had no idea what expression she had worn, and supposed that some explanation was called for, she added, 'That was—Ryan,' and was so knotted up inside that she momentarily forgot that her aunt had answered the phone, so knew quite well who it was. 'He—wants me to go and see him—*now*—would you believe?' She tried to laugh scornfully.

But her aunt saw nothing to laugh at, scornfully or otherwise. Though to Meredith's frustration she did smile, apparently in total agreement with her great nephew-in-law's bossy edicts, as she replied, 'Then you'd better go, Meredith,' and added, 'Take a taxi, dear.' Meredith was staring at her, intending to do nothing of the kind, when happily Evelyn Simmons tacked on, 'There'll be no need for me to wait up tonight—you probably won't be back tonight anyway, come to think of it,' she said on a cheerful afterthought.

'I'll...' Meredith began, and realised that she had just been about to state that she would be back—when in actual fact she had no intention of going anywhere. Only, as her voice faded, she suddenly started to get mutinous again. Dammit, what was she afraid of, that she should refuse to go and see him? Being divorced could not be any worse than what she had now, for goodness' sake! 'I'll go, then, Aunty,' she heard herself say, and, the decision made, she picked up the phone, this time to ring for a taxi.

So he wanted a divorce, did he? she mutinied as she began to dial. Well, far be it from her to stand in his way!

CHAPTER NINE

MEREDITH was still mutinying against Ryan Carlisle when the taxi dropped her off at the smart apartment block where he lived. Nor was her mutiny in any way softened when Preston, the hall security man, greeting her as if he fully remembered her, said, 'Good evening, Mrs Carlisle,' and, as he smartly preceded her to press the lift call button, remarked politely, 'Mr Carlisle is expecting you, madam.'

The over-confident, overbearing swine! she fumed as the lift carried her upwards, her anger increasing by the second that Ryan had been so sure she would jump to his command that he had phoned down to tell security she would be arriving shortly.

She would not jump to his bidding, though, she would not! she thought angrily as she stepped out of the lift. She was here now because *she* wanted a divorce, and the sooner, the better. Ryan had said he was going away tomorrow—what was there to wait for? By the time he came back, she would have consulted her solicitor.

Fleetingly it passed through her mind to consider that perhaps their two solicitors would be the best people to consult rather than each other, but she brushed the thought aside. Before either of them consulted lawyers, they had to agree what grounds to use, didn't they?

A small flutter of nervousness unexpectedly seized her as she reached the apartment door of the man she had married. Angrily she pushed nervousness behind her and, stretching out a finger, even while aware that the ef-

ficient Preston had in all probability telephoned Ryan
to say she was on her way up, she stabbed hard, and
defiantly, at his doorbell.

A few moments later the door was opened. 'Come in,'
he said tersely, his tone as uninviting as his look.

Without a word, her face as unsmiling as his, Meredith
crossed over his threshold and waited politely, if stony-
expressioned, for him to invite her across the hall and
down the three steps into his sitting-room. The sight of
him, tall and casually clad in a summer shirt and trousers,
was already working against her mutiny, though.

Striving to get herself under control after the initial
impact of seeing him, she began to distrust her emotions
when, as his hand came out as though he would guide
her down into his sitting-room, she felt a strange confusion. Deciding against allowing his touch to disrupt
her emotions, she stepped smartly away from him and
went down the steps.

'Take a seat,' Ryan invited coolly as he joined her near
to one of the two couches in the room.

'This shouldn't take long,' she responded, her voice,
she was glad to note, as cool as his. But, since it seemed
sensible to do as he suggested, she took a seat on one
of the couches. She watched as he lowered his length on
to the one opposite, then began, 'You want a divorce,
and...'

'I never said that,' he cut her off before she could
finish.

For a second or two her heart behaved ridiculously,
for Ryan appeared to be saying that he did not want a
divorce. But, casting her mind back to what he had said,
Meredith knew, since he had asked—no, ordered—her
to come so they should discuss their divorce, that

whatever he had or had not said, a divorce was what he wanted.

'Well, I'm not here for the good of my health!' she snapped tartly.

'Hmph, you've changed!' he grunted.

'Was I supposed to stay nice and biddable once I'd got what I wanted?' she retorted, not missing the way his eyes narrowed at her deliberate use of the word 'biddable'.

'You're saying that you really were the phoney I first took you for?' he challenged.

'What else?' Meredith kept a grip on herself to reply. It was something of a revelation to her that Ryan had distrusted her from the beginning. Although, she quickly recalled, it had only taken until their wedding day for the truth of what he believed to be revealed. Firmly she took herself in hand. Ryan must never know the true reason why she had married him. 'You knew I only married you to get away from my family,' she thought there would be no harm in reminding him.

'It doesn't appear to have done you much good, does it?' he rapped, for some reason which was completely obscure to her not seeming to thank her for the reminder.

'Not then,' she replied, and, her tone softening, 'Neither of us knew then that we would soon lose Uncle Porter. But,' she went on brightly, knowing he would remember who Mrs Peplow was, 'yesterday Aunt Evelyn and Mrs Peplow put their properties up for sale. They'll most likely move into a large flat together. Which,' she let him know, 'will leave me as free as air. So all's well that ends well.' She even managed a civilised smile. 'Now, what grounds shall we use for our divorce?'

Ryan did not return her smile. Indeed, it was more of
a glower than a smile she got from him as he said shortly,
'You tell me!'

Which, Meredith thought, was very unfair in the circumstances. He had been around far more than she, so
he must know how these things went. Her smile disappeared and she felt sorely like glowering at him in return,
for, when she thought of how much more he had been
around, it brought to mind that stunning creature he
had been with last night. 'How about—adultery?' she
was driven to ask—but only to be astonished by Ryan's
reaction.

'*Yours?*' he snarled explosively, his expression suddenly murderous.

'Certainly not!' she hurled back in outrage. 'I meant
you!' she said hotly, and was astonished yet again when
not only did his murderous expression abruptly vanish,
but he actually smiled.

'Certainly not me, Meredith,' he told her with some
charm, and, to make her bones melt, 'I haven't looked
at another woman since the day we met.'

'Oh,' she murmured, and did not even recognise that
his charm had just rendered her ready to lie down and
let him walk all over her until, just then, she remembered that it had not been Scotch mist he'd had for
company at the theatre last night! 'Oh!' she said again,
only this time it was said out of sudden fury, not only
with him, but herself. 'Not much you haven't looked at
another woman!' she lashed out waspishly, determining
that never again would she be taken in by him. By no
chance was she going to be led up the garden path twice!
'You'll be telling me next that your *friend* at the theatre
last night was...' she spoke hotly, but was stopped cold

in her tracks when, with his grey eyes searching her
expression, Ryan cut her off.

'You sound—jealous?' he murmured thoughtfully.

Panicking wildly, Meredith scorned, 'Oh, for heaven's
sake!' every bit as if she had never shaken hands with
that green-eyed monster. 'I'm not jealous, I'm just angry
that you can tell such blatant lies when I've seen you
with other women with my own eyes!'

'Correction—woman, in the singular,' Ryan replied,
and, his expression serious, he told her, 'I didn't lie to
you intentionally,' he told her, 'It's just that, apart from
certain innate considerations, with Claudine Benetti
negotiating business with all the toughness of a man, it's
easy to overlook the fact that she's female.'

'Easy?' Meredith queried sceptically, positive, as she
recalled the stunning woman, that Ryan was playing her
for a fool. Before he could answer that question, though,
her recently acquired sarcastic tongue had found another
sceptical question. 'And what would the "certain innate
considerations" be, I wonder?' she scoffed.

Fully expecting him to come back with something short
and pithy on what she could do with her questions *and*
her sarcasm, she was surprised into believing him when
unhesitatingly he replied, 'More—common courtesies to
a female on the board of one of the overseas firms my
company deals with. Claudine had come especially to
do business with us,' he went on. 'When my PA discovered that she'd a liking for musicals, it was not only
courtesy but everyday working practice to entertain her
at the theatre when our business was satisfactorily
concluded.'

'You don't regularly take her to the theatre, then?'
Meredith queried, and wanted to bite her tongue out as
her enchantment at hearing that she had not the slightest

cause for jealousy faded slightly and she realised that for her sanity's sake she must keep her mind on the divorce.

'No, I don't,' he replied, and very nearly melted her bones again when, looking deeply into her eyes, he continued, 'Had my—er—reception—been more favourable when I came to see you on Monday, I'd have asked you to act as hostess for me at the theatre last night.'

'You came to see me on Monday to ask me to...' Her voice petered out, and almost she apologised for the way she had been with him. Almost, but not quite. She had to be tough, otherwise he *would* walk all over her.

'That was part of my reason for coming to see you,' Ryan agreed, without letting her know what the other part was. 'When you lost your temper,' he went on, for all the world as though he was a saint, 'there was nothing for it but for me to accede to your request not to call at your home again, and to ask one of my directors and his wife to make up a four.'

Meredith could not find fault there, or call him a liar, because there had been four people in the box, even if she had been so torn apart by jealousy and pain that she had no memory of what the other two had looked like. But, as her heart rejoiced that she had no need to be jealous of the woman who she now knew was called Claudine Benetti, so Meredith again had to find some toughness in herself. It had gladdened her heart that Ryan had called at her home because he had wanted her to act as his hostess. More, she was positively thrilled that it should have occurred to him to ask her. But was she to be such a weakling that she swooned with every magical, wonderful word that fell from his lips? His devious, enchanting but entirely self-motivated lips, her saner self prodded.

'Well, we both know that you'd do anything when it concerns business, don't we?' she exclaimed acidly, and only just held back from making some sarcastic reference to the fact that she would not be in his apartment now, waiting to discuss their divorce, had he not prized his business above his bachelorhood.

Ryan, though, had quickly picked up the acid in her tone, and Meredith realised that she must not only be stronger where he was concerned, but more careful too, when, with a more gentle note in his voice, he asked, 'Did I hurt you, Meredith, when I married you for those shares?'

'Of course not,' she lied promptly. 'Though I'd have appreciated a little more honesty from you before we got that far,' she added, and realised, belatedly, that she had left herself wide open to be challenged—what about her honesty in pretending to care for him in order to get away from her elderly relatives?

He did nothing of the kind, however, but, accepting full blame for his actions, he owned, 'I could have been more honest, I agree. I was wary, though,' he owned, and explained, 'There was I, with the shares in Burgess Electrical having dried to a trickle, searching all routes to find some way of ultimately being in a position to control that firm. Then one day, straight out of the blue, and without so much as a word of prompting on my part, a beautiful and totally unknown young woman bearing the name-tag Miss M. Maybry buttonholes me to blurt out that her father had left her thousands and thousands of the precise shares I'm desperate to get my hands on.'

Meredith sailed briefly up on a see-saw of delight to hear Ryan describe her as beautiful, only to plummet speedily at his factual 'buttonholes me'. Though since, in order to be strong, she thought it better to keep away from anything personal, she opted to keep her questions as impersonal as possible.

'You thought there was something fishy?' she asked.

'Wouldn't you, given the same circumstances?' he countered.

'Well, it didn't stop you from finding out where I lived and what my telephone number was, did it?' she retorted, her face unsmiling.

'Neither was too difficult to discover,' he replied calmly. 'Though, to be accurate, it was Monte Montgomery who set the wheels in motion to trace you, not I.'

Meredith did not like what she was hearing one little bit. 'The two of you wanted control of Burgess Electrical?' she questioned, remembering that Monte Montgomery had known, when she had not, that Ryan had married her for her shares, 'Confound it, Ryan,' she exclaimed, 'the pair of you must have laughed yourselves silly behind my back!'

'Don't be ridiculous, it wasn't like that!' he retorted sharply.

'Like hell it wasn't!' Meredith flew. But although she was feeling angry enough, and hurt enough, to march straight out of Ryan's apartment, she suddenly checked. She must not take everything he said so much to heart— she must not. She had to appear as if nothing he could say would hurt her. He must not gain so much as a hint of the extent of her caring for him. Yet, if she did not take control of her feelings and keep everything on that impersonal basis she was looking for, then he was much too clever to miss how things were with her. 'So,' she said, having gathered some control and hoping to make him believe she had just been taking what he said apart, 'why not tell me, if it wasn't "like that", how it really was?'

'I should like to,' he said simply, and when she had begun to doubt he would, he accepted her challenge and began. 'You'd spoken to me of your shares that Friday, as I mentioned, and I was still trying to work out what your angle was when later that day Monte Montgomery rang to thank me for my support at the opening.'

'An . . .' Meredith had been going to challenge his use of the word 'angle', but as she recalled that he thought she was ready to use the bait of her shares to get away from her relatives, she quickly changed what she had been going to say. 'Monte Montgomery rang to thank you for your support?' she queried—when she was not the slightest interested in Monte Montgomery.

'Believe it or not, even the most confident of us get nervous on some occasions,' Ryan replied quietly, his grey eyes steady on hers.

'I'll—believe it,' she mumbled, and he went on.

'Since Monte knew all about my aspirations regarding Burgess Electrical, it seemed only natural to tell him of my amazing encounter with you.'

'What did he say?' she asked, accepting that his amazement stemmed from the fact that, with everyone chasing around for Burgess Electrical shares, there she had been suddenly announcing that her father had left her thousands and thousands of them.

'Like me, he too wondered what your angle was. Though he was of the view that you'd read somewhere how most firms in the electronics field were showing an interest in Burgess Electrical,' Ryan replied. 'He thought, however, that it might be worthwhile getting in touch with his window-dressing section. In no time at all he had been on to some agency, and was back on the phone to me again.'

'This time to give you my address and phone number?'

'Precisely,' Ryan agreed, but without knowing it he made her heart race a little when he went on, 'I couldn't get you out of my mind the whole of that Friday night. Again and again, your face would come back to haunt me.'

A small sighing sound escaped her, but rapidly Meredith collected herself and got herself more of a piece. 'Well, it would,' she said, complimenting herself that in the circumstances her voice should come out sounding so even. 'Here was your chance to get your hands on those shares—if, of course, you played your cards right.' Her even tone started to falter, but she quickly dragged it back, as she reminded him, 'You made use of my phone number the next day, and rang asking me out to dinner.'

'And spent a good part of that dinner wondering if you really were as innocent as you looked and if I should tell you that the value of your shares had gone through the roof recently.'

'You decided against telling me, quite obviously,' Meredith put in.

'Let's say that my better judgement prevailed,' he commented, and, looking at him, Meredith was struck by the fact that his remark was not in any way boastful, but seemed to be said in a more self-derisory fashion than anything else. 'By then, of course, I'd been introduced to your family.'

'Hmm,' she took up, fully intent that he should not wander off the right track. 'That's when you realised what my "angle" was. You realised, almost at once, that I shouldn't at all mind living somewhere apart from my elderly relatives?'

Ryan nodded. 'If,' he qualified on her behalf, 'it could be done without causing them any pain.'

'You knew, then,' she made her face blank as she queried, 'that I was ready to marry you as a way out?'

'You didn't waste any time in telling me that those shares went to your husband on your wedding day,' Ryan confirmed.

'It's a wonder to me, what with you wanting those shares so badly,' Meredith said coolly, 'that you didn't propose to me on our first date!' Oh, lord, she thought, when Ryan gave her a sharp look, I'm getting personal again. 'Ah!' she said brightly, as hurriedly getting away from the personal. 'You hadn't seen proof then that my father had any shares to leave, much less that, as I'd told you, my husband was to inherit them if I married before my twenty-fifth birthday.'

'You were kind enough to "accidentally" leave the papers I needed in my car the second time we went out,' Ryan smiled, and Meredith smiled too because, quite plainly, he believed she had left the file containing the share certificates and her father's will in his car on purpose so that he could check them out. When in actual fact she had clean forgotten about the file until later. 'It soon became clear, since there appeared to be no way in which I could purchase those shares from you, that I was going to have to marry you,' he said, causing Meredith to have trouble with her smile.

'It's so tough at the top!' she said acidly, and thought, terrified, that she had completely blown her cover when Ryan looked at her sharply.

'Have I really hurt you so much?' he questioned quickly.

'Hurt me?' she scorned. 'Good grief, Ryan, you know better than that!'

Strangely, and to her surprise, he seemed more disgruntled by her reply than pleased, and he went on harshly as if he had suddenly got tired of telling her 'how it really was'. 'Once everything checked out,' he told her coolly, 'I again got on to Monte. You didn't look twenty, but if you were already twenty-five I'd have lost out on the deal.'

'And you couldn't have that!' she inserted, the pain he had caused her and was still causing her chipping away at the hard covering she was trying to protect herself with.

'No, I couldn't,' he agreed. 'I'm a businessman. For my company's future, I wanted those shares at any price. When I told Monte why I wanted to know your age, and he reported back that the agency records gave your age as twenty-two, he also advised that I shouldn't drag my feet. I invited him there and then to be my best man.'

'Before you'd asked me to marry you!' Meredith exclaimed, but quickly concealed her resentment that he should be so sure of her by saying evenly, 'though I suppose it was a foregone conclusion that I'd accept.'

'I thought so,' he replied. 'Though, frankly, I did feel some disquiet the first time I kissed you.'

'My apologies,' Meredith said drily, and loved him with all that was in her when he laughed as though she had amused him.

And then, quite electrifyingly, he said quietly, 'I think, Meredith, that that was the moment when you first started to get to me.'

'I did—what?' she asked chokily. But even while her heart began to race, scepticism was at work in her. She would not be led on a false trail—she would not. 'Oh, you mean because I—er—didn't seem to have been kissed before, or have too much experience of men?' she followed up aloofly.

'You hadn't *any* experience of men,' Ryan corrected, starting to look a little tough at her tone. 'But yes,' he admitted, 'that was part of it. And since it seemed you wanted a little romance in your life, I was prepared to play my part there too. Th...'

'How benevolent of you!' Meredith could not resist saying, and was ignored for her trouble.

'But everything seemed so easy,' he continued.

'Well, it was, wasn't it?' she tossed in, seemingly uncaringly. 'I needed an out, you needed the shares—the two fitted together perfectly.'

'*Too* perfectly!' clipped Ryan. 'As I was very soon to discover, there *had* to be a catch.'

'A catch?'

He nodded, and, looking at him, Meredith was reminded of his saying only a short time ago that even the most confident of men sometimes felt nervous. Because somehow Ryan, who had never been anything other than confident, suddenly seemed—as if he was a little unsure of his ground!

Shrugging away the notion as fantasy, she heard his voice as strong and as terrific as ever when he began to document, 'I'd thought it out all very carefully beforehand. I'd looked into every aspect of any marriage between us—or so I thought—and couldn't see any one problem that I couldn't handle. My bride, as I perceived her, was a young woman who, as well as being sweet, was, as you overheard me telling Monte, biddable into the bargain.'

'As you said,' Meredith murmured, keeping the tightest rein on her tongue, 'no problem.'

'Exactly,' he agreed. 'Were you ever to become a problem, though, or tiresome in any way, then I had the answer to that too. Quite easily,' he went on to openly admit, 'I would get a divorce.'

'Hmm,' Meredith murmured, as she tried to appear completely relaxed on the couch she was sitting on, when in actual fact she was suddenly as tense as a tautly strung bow. Because here, at last, with that word 'divorce', they had reached the purpose of her visit to Ryan's apartment. She somehow managed a smile, though, as she queried, 'I still don't see where the "catch" is?'

'It began, my dear Meredith,' he said softly, his word his tone, threatening to ruin her determination never again to be weak, 'when, before we'd been married twenty-four hours, you were taking a furious swipe at me, and showing me quite clearly that I'd made the most serious misjudgement of character when I'd called you biddable.'

'I'm not sorry I hit you!' she found some stiffening to tell him hostilely.

'I deserved that slap, and more,' he undermined her again by agreeing with her. 'And more was what I got too,' he said slowly, 'when instead of telephoning you in Little Haversham to tell you your uncle was ill, I found myself making the journey to Derbyshire to come for you personally.'

'But you were in Derbyshire anyway—on business!'

'I agreed with you that I had business in the area,' Ryan replied, 'but I came especially—for you.'

With her blue eyes widening as she stared at him, all
Meredith could hope as her heart suddenly gave the most
tremendous surge of energy was that she would give none
of her inner feelings away.

'You came because you believed my uncle to be most
seriously ill?' she queried quietly.

'I came because, despite what I might at that time
have been telling myself to the contrary, there had
awakened in me a need—to see—you.'

Swiftly Meredith looked away from him. Oh, dear
heaven, if only it was true that Ryan had felt a need to
see her! But common sense soon quieted the wild clam-
ourings of her heart. Had she not been ecstatic once
before—on her wedding day, if memory served—only to
receive the biggest let-down of her life a very short while
later? It was not going to happen again, she resolved.
Whatever Ryan said, she must listen to him with her head
and not her heart.

'As I remember it, you didn't seem very pleased to
see me,' she remarked as coolly as she was able.

'I was still mentally kicking myself for making the
journey,' he said evenly, his eyes fixed on hers as he
reminded her, 'As I recall it, your greeting to me was
not over-effusive.'

The cheek of him! Meredith fumed. After the way he
had shattered her dreams, he thought she should have
been all over him! She bit hard on the angry retort that
sprang to her lips, though, when caution prompted her
that Ryan had had no idea of the dreams she had woven.

'There was no need for me to pretend any more,
surely?' she queried, and left him to work out that, since
they had both got what they wanted, she had no need
to pretend that she even liked him if she did not want
to.

'Perhaps not,' he replied stiffly. 'I was merely your husband. Not,' he said succinctly, 'your kissing friend.'

The nerve of him! Meredith thought, yet again, that he really was the limit. 'You can't make anything out of my friendship with Tessa's brother,' she told him shortly as it suddenly occurred to her that Ryan might in some obscure way be leading up to citing Aldo in his divorce petition.

'You've no feelings for him, other than those of a friend?' clipped Ryan, his eyes suddenly burning into hers as if the answer really meant something to him.

'No!' Meredith answered sharply, and because it upset her that he looked to be ready to soil her name to get his freedom, 'I might have had a crush on Aldo in my teens, but I was over that the one and only time that he kissed me on the mouth,' she told him woodenly—and was amazed at Ryan's reply.

'Thank the lord for that,' he said, and seemed so sincere that Meredith knew she must have got it wrong and that he had never meant to couple Aldo's name with hers in the divorce courts.

'That sounded rather heartfelt,' she remarked, and wished with all she had that she knew what sort of game Ryan was playing, when he said,

'It was heartfelt! You can have no idea of the jealousy I've had to endure on account of your friend's brother.'

'Jealousy!' she exclaimed, and could only stare, and wonder at her husband's powers of invention.

'I didn't know the meaning of the word jealousy until suddenly there you were introducing this man Wallace, who called you "pet", and who kissed you goodbye,' he told her. Remembering clearly how, when she'd introduced Aldo, Ryan had spoken to him curtly, and had seemed to have no time for him, Meredith felt her emotions were on a merry-go-round when Ryan, his manner wry, went on, 'And, if it wasn't enough that you should awaken that serpent jealousy in me, then, when all along I'd counted it as entirely my prerogative to make the decision with regard to a divorce, in less than no time you steal my thunder by talking to me about "when we divorce".'

'Shame!' Meredith mocked as she again took severe charge of the putty-like person she would be in his hands if she didn't do something about it. And even though she could tell from the sudden glint in his eyes that Ryan was finding her mockery very difficult to swallow, she went on to drawl insolently, 'We seem to have taken a very roundabout route, but at last we're back to the beginning. You want a divorce, and I . . .'

'That's just it,' he stopped her in her tracks, but paused, and again seemed nervous, before he added bluntly, 'I don't want a divorce!'

'You don't want . . . But . . . That's why I'm here!' she recovered from being winded to complete a sentence. 'I'm here to discuss . . .'

'You're here because I want, and need, and, quite simply, *have* to talk to you uninterrupted,' Ryan cut her off.

'You have—do you?' Meredith questioned warily, as she wondered which garden path he was taking her up this time.

'I do,' he confirmed, and set her heart thumping when, as if the space between them was too great, he moved quickly and before she knew it had come to share the couch on which she was sitting. 'I do,' he said again, and as she looked at him anxiously, 'Don't be afraid, Meredith,' he told her gently. 'If I've hurt you in the past, then I swear I'll never hurt you again.'

Sorely then did she need to scoff that, for goodness' sake, she had never been hurt by him for a moment. But the words to put any such idea out of his mind would not come, and she was left having to scrape up what intelligence his nearness had left her with, and to question, 'You—er—need to talk to me because you—er—don't want a divorce?'

'How I do *not* want a divorce,' Ryan said softly, and when she just stared at him, he went on, 'How or when you started to weave your spell over me, whether before our wedding day or afterwards, I cannot tell. Wh...'

'Spell?' she whispered.

'Yes, my dear,' Ryan breathed, and gently took her two hands in his as he told her, 'I don't know how or when; all I know is that, as suddenly as you came into my life, with hurricane force you were gone from it. And I,' he said quietly, 'discovered that I didn't like it.'

'You didn't like my—er—hitting you?' she asked chokily, thinking he must be calling the strength of her slap to his face a 'hurricane force'.

'I didn't like you leaving, sweet Meredith,' he replied, his grey eyes warm and serious on hers. 'I had told you that you were your own person now,' he continued, and had her staring at him open-mouthed when he ended, 'but when images of you began to penetrate my thoughts at all times of the night and day, I had to face the fact that anything you did as your own person from now on, I wanted to include me.'

'You're—not serious?' she just had to ask, when she could see for herself how serious he looked.

'I've never been more serious in my life,' he told her, and confessed, 'I hadn't wanted a wife, but, since I needed those shares badly enough to take a wife with them, a divorce seemed a most satisfactory outcome in due time. The catch, which I hadn't foreseen,' Ryan went on, 'was that I should start to miss my wife, and that, in missing this woman who had so recently become a part of my life, I should realise, when time and again I wanted to see her, how very much attracted to her I had become.' Meredith's attention was riveted on him when he brought out, 'The catch was that, ultimately, I had to accept that a divorce was the very last thing I wanted.'

'Oh,' Meredith said on a gossamer breath, and she very nearly smiled, and she was very nearly ready to do whatever he asked of her. Just in time, though, she re-called—with something of a jolt—the charm Ryan had used one evening when he had said to her 'You'd better marry me, without delay' and she had asked 'You love me?' He had never answered that question, and she had been foolish enough to believe that she had no need to put such a question to him anyway. But that was then—and this was now. It seemed to her then, though, that she would have only herself to blame if she asked the same question so foolishly a second time. However, if Ryan was as sincere as he would have her believe—then what were a few other questions between friends? But, because the feel of his skin against hers as he gripped on to her hands was doing nothing to aid her power of clear thinking, she hurriedly pulled her hands out of his hold. 'Forgive me, Ryan, if it seems that I've no great trust in y-your remarks,' she managed then, 'but, if I might be allowed to recap...'

'Ask anything you want to ask, and I shall answer honestly.' Ryan, she saw, seemed eager to have every one of her doubts brought out into the open.

'You said you came to Little Haversham that first time, especially to see me?'

'And the second time too,' he startled her by confessing.

'But—you had an elderly relative living that way; you told me you...'

'I lied,' he interrupted her gently.

'But you're not lying now?'

'I've done with lies and pretence,' he replied promptly.

'I see,' Meredith murmured, but she knew she was merely playing for time, because she could not see anything at all—and she was so desperately afraid. All her instincts were urging her to go along with everything he said, to believe he had no intention of telling her another lie. But, on his own admittance, he had lied to her before.

'I don't think you do see,' he said quietly. 'At least, if you do see, you're determined not to trust, nor to believe that you have me so much at sixes and sevens that I barely know where the hell I'm heading.'

'I seem to have—er—quite some—er—p-power over you,' she stammered, having meant it to come out sarcastically but discovering that there was not a shadow of sarcasm in her voice. And Ryan took her stammered comment seriously, when he replied,

'And then some! Without my even knowing it, something about you had started to get to me. I'd seen you sweet and gentle with your elderly relatives. Patient with your uncle, and guardian to him one early morning when, having spent the most restless night of my life in your bed, I came to your uncle's room to find you.'

'I don't think I could be called much of a guardian to him.' Meredith, on the lookout for further lies, found some will to oppose him.

'You were asleep when I came in to say I was going,' Ryan admitted, and defeated her opposition in one fell swoop when he added, 'You were asleep, and lovely, and as I looked down at you something so unexpectedly tender came over me that I just had to kiss your brow before I left.'

'I—w-woke up,' Meredith remembered, her voice more than a degree wobbly. That was before she recalled what had taken place only a very short while later. 'And I suppose you "just had to kiss me", too, when I went to the front door with you to see you out!' she exclaimed tartly. And, rushing on regardless of his surprised look at her harsh change of tone, 'Your kissing me then had nothing at all to do with the fact that Aunt Evelyn was standing there watching, I take it,' she added, and could have crowned him yet at the same time thrown herself into his arms when a smile of utter charm broke on his well-shaped mouth.

'Oh, Meredith—Meredith,' he breathed. 'I kissed you then, little love, because you were smiling so sweetly at me and I found you totally irresistible. I kissed you because I wanted to, and discovered that it was like kissing you for the first time. It was only after I kissed you that I saw your aunt,' he informed her. 'And at that time I was glad she was there, because I was striving for sanity and realising that I had made the right decision when, before I left your bedroom, I faced the fact that I needed to get away to try and get things into perspective.'

For a moment or two Meredith was too dumbstruck to say a word. Then, haltingly, while hating her weakness in asking, she just had to question, 'Did you g-get things into perspective?'

'Did I hell!' Ryan gritted, thrilling her. 'Logic was suddenly a thing of the past. I'd left you early that morning because I needed to think, and spent the rest of the day wanting to come back to you.'

'But you didn't.'

'I told myself I was being a fool,' he said, a self-derisory smile quirking his mouth. 'Which of course didn't stop me doing the next best thing.'

'You telephoned,' Meredith supplied.

'And you let me know—since I was supposed to be flying off somewhere that night—that you didn't want to hear from me for two weeks.'

'That's—true,' she said, refraining from telling him how much she had wished she had not said that.

'So can you wonder that I'm furious when, having spent over a week fighting the compulsion to ring you, when I do give in, as give in I must, I discover that you aren't cosily ensconced in your family home as I'd supposed, but cosily ensconced up in Little Haversham with your friend—and, for all I knew, your friend's amorous brother.'

'Amorous!' Meredith exclaimed, while wondering if her heart would ever beat normally again.

'Did I not mention that I've discovered myself a jealous man?' Ryan queried, and Meredith knew then that if she didn't take a firm hold on the situation, his charm was going to sink her.

'Yes, you did,' she said as coolly as she was able. 'Jealousy, instigated by my being friends with Aldo and...'

'And which friendship brought matters to a head for me last night,' Ryan quietly cut in.

'How?' she asked, wanting to run, wanting to stay, but above all trying to bury her instincts under the intelligence of her head.

'It was more than enough to have me want to physically rearrange his features when I saw that he was daring to escort *my wife* to the theatre,' Ryan replied. 'When, with him only yards away, you told me you wanted a divorce, to merely render him temporarily unconscious seemed mild to the murderous tendencies that awakened in me then. But, while I was able to outwardly conceal my inner feelings, I later knew that I'd have to take some action, or I would go demented for sure.'

'Which—is why you telephoned me tonight?'

'Which is why I rang and asked you to come where we could talk unhindered,' Ryan agreed, his phrasing, to Meredith's ears, slightly different from the way she remembered the telephone conversation going. 'Thoughts of you have had me sleepless more times than I care to remember,' he went on, 'last night having no equal. I've thought, eaten, dreamt you, Meredith Carlisle,' he told her. 'And seemed to have spent half of my life trying not to pick up the phone to ring you. But tonight, before I rang, I just knew that I couldn't endure another night without taking that action.'

Her breath caught in her throat, and Meredith desperately needed help from somewhere. But she was in this alone, and where her instincts were concerned she had learned a very hard lesson, a painful lesson. Indeed, she could still feel the pain from learning that Ryan had married her, not from love, but because of those shares. 'Ah!' she exclaimed when, on thinking of those shares, all her logic banded together to tell her that, whatever Ryan was up to now, it just had to have something to do with those shares. 'Those shares,' she said suddenly, and ploughed on through his look of surprise that she should bring them up when they had not been discussing them. '*Your* shares,' she corrected. 'Th...'

'They're not mine any longer,' he told her, and as it sank in that he must have sold them and—if the price he got was anything like the price she'd seen quoted—they must have realised a tremendous amount, Meredith went cold from head to foot. 'With everything else happening, I forgot...' Ryan broke off, but even as he said, 'Just a minute...' and went swiftly from the couch to stride across the carpet and up the three steps to disappear round the hall in the direction of the bedrooms, Meredith lost interest.

It was not the money. In fact, she didn't care then that Ryan must have done a deal which had netted him a colossal sum. It was the fact that he had deceived her yet again. She had no experience whatsoever of what went on with regard to the stock market, but as she heard movements indicating that Ryan must be looking for something, she was somehow sure that she was about to be beguiled again. How it was to be done, she had no idea. Why, since he had admitted to having sold his holdings in Burgess Electrical, she knew even less. All she did know, however, was that Ryan for some reason didn't want a divorce, and that towards that end, though of course without actually committing himself, he had, for some nefarious business reason of his own, been trying to get her to think he had some feeling for her.

Struggling hard not to cry out in her anguish at having nearly been taken in a second time, Meredith was on her feet when, with a folder in his hands, Ryan came swiftly back into the room.

He seemed to take the three steps down into the sitting-room in one as he noted that she was standing and that she had a set expression on her face. 'Here it...' he began.

'Goodbye, Ryan,' she said frigidly, and as she realised she should have done over the phone, 'My solicitors will be in touch,' she told him icily.

'Your solicitors!' he exclaimed, for all the world as though he had no clue to what she was talking of.

'About the divorce,' she told him hotly, and went to march across the carpet.

As she went to pass him though his hand shot out and he caught hold of her and spun her round. 'Divorce...' he grated, and Meredith knew that there must be something peculiar about the lighting in his flat, for he seemed to have lost some of his colour as he demanded, 'Have you not heard a word of what I've been saying?'

'I've heard every single word,' she replied, her nails biting into her palms as she fought for control. She had to get away. She had to go, and go now.

'It means nothing to you?' he retained his firm hold on her to ask, a hoarse note she could not allow herself to believe in coming to his voice. 'None of what I've said...'

'Means a thing to me,' Meredith told him, only by sheer effort of will managing to keep her tone hostile.

'You can't mean that!' he exploded. 'I thought... You seemed...'

'Would you mind very much taking your hand off my arm!' she told him coolly. 'I want to leave.'

'But you can't go!' he said in an anguished tone. 'I won't let you go!'

Oh, dear heaven, Meredith thought, and knew that if she did not get away now, he truly would walk all over her. 'What's the matter, Ryan,' she found enough strength to make a final effort, 'can't you take it when things don't map out the way you want them?' Watching through eyes which she was doing her hardest to keep cool and in keeping with her sarcastic tone, she saw a muscle move in his temple and observed that he seemed to be making gigantic efforts to get himself together. 'Do take your hand off me, there's a dear,' she went on to

drawl. 'As you once said, I'm my own person now—
and this person wants to go home.'

To her utter relief, she had no need to say more. Ryan
dropped his hand from her and, as though seeking to
grasp at what control he could muster, he abruptly turned
his back on her. Meredith turned too, in the opposite
direction, and made rapidly for the steps that led to the
hall.

Tears were stinging her eyes as she negotiated the three
steps, and although she felt certain that he would not
come after her, a flutter of panic made her take a side-
step along the hall. When she was out of his line of
vision, should he have turned about, she brushed an
emotional stray tear from her eye, and was about to head
for the apartment door when, for some unknown reason,
she flicked a glance to the right and along the hall. Ab-
sently she took in the fact that Ryan had been in such
a hurry to get back to her with that folder that he had
left his bedroom door open.

Her glance was still on the wide-open bedroom door
when she noticed something that was to instantly dry
any tears that might have been held back waiting to be
shed.

The swine! she fumed. The unmitigated, treacherous
swine! For there on his bedside table, positioned to face
his bed, stood a picture in a frame. Fury like none she
had ever known hit Meredith then. And as that fury
raged in her and mingled hotly with jealousy, she went
storming into the bedroom and snatched up the picture.

Quite what she intended to do with it she was not absolutely sure, though the desire to hit him over the head
with it for being able to talk as though lovingly to her
while he had the picture of some other woman on his
bedside came near to the top of the list.

But that was only until, expecting to see the face of Claudine Benetti, or someone sophisticated and beautiful like her, Meredith looked down at the framed picture in her hands. And then, as the world started to spin, she almost fainted from shock.

She did not faint. But as incredulity became credulity, she moved. With her heart banging away against her ribs, she went slowly from Ryan's bedroom and along the hall, until she was standing on the top of the steps. The folder that had been in his hand had been tossed down on to a low table near to one of the couches, but Ryan himself, still with his back to her, had moved to a drinks cabinet and appeared to be pouring himself a stiff drink.

'Ryan!' she called, and saw him freeze. Then she saw the bottle go down, and then the glass, and he turned. His expression by then, though, was a chiselled mask, and Meredith had an idea that this was how he would look when he was at his most unapproachable. She weathered his grim, steely-eyed scrutiny, but when he had not a word to say her courage momentarily faltered. She had the framed picture in her hands, though, and even if she still could not quite believe it, another glance at the laughing and carefree face sketched there made her grasp at courage and hold out the picture to him. 'Where—did you get this?' she asked him huskily.

For a moment she thought that Ryan was not going to answer. But, as though he had just sensed how vitally important her discovery of that picture by his bedside was, answer her he did, albeit curtly.

'I stole it.'

'Fr-from Tessa's kitchen dresser?' Meredith asked, nerves getting to her, because she already knew from where he had stolen it.

'While you went upstairs to get a jacket,' he confirmed, the gravity of his features remaining unchanged.

'Why?' she just had to ask then. And, when it seemed as if he thought he had told her all he was going to tell her, she pleaded, 'Please, Ryan, won't you tell me why you stole it, why you had it framed, and wh-why you wanted a picture of me on your bedside table?'

'I'm not in the habit of repeating myself,' he replied at long last. 'I've already told you why.'

Meredith's voice had dried up, but she regained it, only for her words to come out sounding more husky than ever when she told him, 'No, you haven't—actually.'

'I—haven't?' he enquired slowly.

She shook her head and, with her eyes fixed on his, she thought she saw that an alert look had come to his eyes as she asked, 'Couldn't you—just this once—repeat what you think I should have heard, but haven't?'

His answer was to take several strides towards her, as though he needed to read in return what there was in her eyes to be read. He stopped, though, somewhere in the middle of the carpet. 'It's—important to you?' he queried.

Meredith swallowed hard. 'Very,' she whispered, and nearly crumpled when the words she had been aching to hear, but never thought that she would, were suddenly there, floating from him to her.

'Then, dammit,' he rapped, 'I love you.'

'That,' said Meredith, as she stepped down one carpeted step, and then another, 'is quite the most wonderful thing you've ever said to me.'

'You—love me?' he questioned tensely.

Meredith nodded. 'Ever since I first saw you,' she confessed shyly, and, hearing his shout of elation, had no memory whatsoever of stepping down the last step.

She had memory only of Ryan coming for her and of being tightly enfolded in his arms as if he would never let her go. Then she had a sensation of minutes happily ticking by as they clung, and just clung to each other. Then his lips were over hers in a kiss of pure bliss and, still in his arms, she discovered that they were on one of the couches, with the picture she had held now down on the table to the side of them. Then, and only then, did they find space to talk.

'Oh, my little love!' Ryan breathed, and seemed to be having some trouble convincing himself that it was as she had said it was. 'Can it be true—that you love me?'

'I fell in love with you at first sight,' Meredith told him, never happier, and having the same sort of trouble herself.

'At that lift at...'

'Before that,' she said, and explained, 'I'd seen you at the opening ceremony, and I knew then, before I'd even spoken with you. That's why—later—at the lift, I just found myself speaking to you.'

'Oh, dear love,' he breathed. 'You're sure?' he questioned.

'I'm sure I'm in love with you, if that's what you're asking,'she told him. 'Though at the time I couldn't believe it. I went along to the staff rest-room to get over the shock, but it was when I decided that I'd better go home that I saw you at the staff lift.'

'And you still felt the same?' he asked, stretching out a hand to gently trace the curve of her face.

Meredith nodded, and she smiled as she told him, 'I've never accosted anyone in my life, yet before I knew it, there I was babbling on about my interests in the electrical field.'

'I'm so glad you did,' Ryan smiled, and with his hand still gentle on the side of her face, he leaned forward and tenderly kissed her, long and lingeringly.

'Oh,' she sighed when their lips parted, and her heart hammered away within her at what he could do to her. 'I know that it wasn't so immediate with you, but when did you...' Her voice tailed away, but it seemed that Ryan knew exactly what she was asking.

'All the signs were there that you were getting to me in a big way,' he told her lovingly, 'but I knew most definitely that I was in love with you on the night we shared your bed.'

'You knew then?' she queried.

'I knew then,' he confirmed, touching his lips to the side of her face when a faint flush of pink coloured her cheeks. 'I hadn't meant to stay in your bedroom with you, as you know, my shy darling,' he said adoringly. 'Neither had I meant to make love to you. At least,' he qualified as he gently kissed her again, 'thoughts of our making love were not in my head when I decided it was absolutely nonsensical for me to go through hell on that small chair in your bedroom while you had half a bed going spare. Anyhow,' he went on, 'in your anguish over your uncle you were restless in your sleep, and I had the most overwhelming need to try to comfort you. It seemed only the natural thing to do to take you in my arms.'

'I woke up once, and found myself in your arms,' Meredith told him.

'I know,' Ryan murmured.

'You know—knew!'

'I felt you go rigid in my hold, and knew you were awake and probably scared, so I thought it best for you to sort out for yourself that you'd come to no harm. All I wanted to do then was to hold and comfort you, though not from any sexual motive. It was then that I knew I was most definitely in love with you. The wonder of it was still with me when you later woke up, and what happened seemed meant to happen, only, on my part, with love.'

'Oh, Ryan,' Meredith sighed, 'it was the same for me too. But...'

'But?' he took up, wanting nothing held back, not now.

'But later I got to thinking that you'd made love to me, not from love, but because you had to be the boss. I thought,' she went on, 'in the days that followed, that, having had me "biddable" in bed, you had no further interest.'

'Great Scott!' he exclaimed, and stared at her in wonder at the way her thoughts had gone. 'I was aching to hold you in my arms again,' he told her. 'But you'd told me not to touch you, and I thought you must be going through some kind of guilt feelings that while your uncle was dying, you'd forgotten everything when the needs of your body were awakened.'

It was Meredith's turn to stare. 'Really?' she gasped, realising that Ryan was far more sensitive than she had given him credit for. 'Is that why...?'

'My heart was aching for you, my darling,' he gently cut in. 'And each time I saw you I had a tremendous yearning to take you in my arms. Yet each time, rather than upset you with everything going on about your Uncle Porter, I managed to hide my feelings. By then I wanted desperately to bring you back here with me. I came specially to discuss our future one day, but...'

'But I told you I'd nothing to discuss with you!' Meredith remembered with more surprise. 'Though you did agree with me when I told you I would stay with my aunt,' she said quietly.

'Until we could make some arrangement to ensure that she wasn't left on her own now her brother had gone, I couldn't do anything else but agree,' Ryan told her. 'It was out of respect for your recent bereavement,' he revealed, 'that I had to let you walk away from me that afternoon when you reminded me of your recent loss by saying you'd return to sorting out your uncle's belongings. Though it was on remembering our conversation that afternoon, and how you'd told me that, if you'd ever been so idiotic as to have some caring for me, it would never have survived what you'd found out on our wedding day, that I began to hope.'

'Did I give myself away?'

Ryan smiled. 'Only in so much as, when I microscopically sifted through my knowledge of you, and of your endearing ways, I discovered that it just didn't tie up that, had you sincerely cared, you could be so fickle as to turn so immediately into someone who didn't care. The Meredith I thought I was beginning to know was the true sort who, once having given her heart, would give it forever. I, my darling, have spent this long day in an agony of uncertainty and hope.'

'Oh, Ryan!' Meredith cried, and as he hauled her close up to him they kissed, and kissed some more, until gently he pulled back from her.

'I think we've both known a little bit of hell, sweetheart,' he said. 'But, for my sanity's sake, do you mind if I don't kiss you again until I've cleared up every last whisper of anything I've ever done that has upset you?'

'I'm sure there's nothing else,' she smiled shyly.

'Forward baggage!' he grinned, and seemed utterly enchanted when she burst out laughing.

'The time we've wasted,' Meredith smiled, as she thought back over the weeks since her uncle had died.

'I thought it best to keep out of the way while you adjusted to your uncle's death,' Ryan owned. 'Though, had I met with a better reception on Monday, to have you act as my hostess to a visiting foreign buyer was to have been the start of my campaign to woo you.'

'Honestly!' she gasped. 'Oh, Ryan,' she mourned. 'And I told you that not only did I neither want to see you nor talk to you, but I didn't need you!'

'And I witnessed at first hand what a demon of a temper my biddable little wife has,' he smiled. 'You didn't mean any of it, did you?' he teased.

'I lied,' she confessed.

'As I lied when, to get you over here, I told you I was going away tomorrow.'

'You're not!'

He shook his head. 'Were you in any small way jealous of Claudine Benetti, by the way?' he wanted to know.

'I slipped up, didn't I?' Meredith said sheepishly.

'I thought I'd glimpsed a touch of green in your eye at the theatre last night. When I wasn't in a lather from my own jealousy of your companion, I took quite some heart at the idea that you might be jealous of mine.'

'Well, whoever would expect a woman as stunning as that to be on the board of some business or other?' Meredith excused herself, and was quite mystified when Ryan suddenly leaned to the table and picked up the folder lying there, and then asked,

'Have you looked in the mirror recently?' And, when she looked at him blankly, 'You're more than a little stunning yourself, Meredith, yet I'd say you've enough shares here to warrant you a seat on the board of Burgess Electrical.'

She opened her mouth in puzzlement, then closed it again. '*I* have?' she questioned, not taking in at all what he was telling her, although there was some vague memory tugging at her of him saying earlier something about those shares no longer being his.

'I feel sure that your father always meant you to have these shares,' Ryan told her, and added as he looked with love down into her bewildered eyes, 'If you'd care to take a glance inside this folder, you'll see that I've had all the shares transferred to your name.'

'But—but ... But those shares go to my husband on the day I marry ...'

'There's nothing in your father's will that says your husband can't have them transferred back into your new name, Meredith Carlisle,' Ryan smiled.

'But—but you wanted them!'

'I discovered that I wanted your love and trust more,' he replied gently. 'If you want to vote your shares with me when the time is ripe, you can. But you don't have to. The decision,' he said, 'is all yours.'

Looking at him, her eyes were filled with her emotion. 'Oh, Ryan,' she said on a breath of sound, 'I do so love you.'

'I'm glad about that,' he said softly, and tenderly he enfolded her in his arms and kissed her.

Many long minutes passed, but finally they drew apart, when Meredith, slightly delirious from his kisses, murmured, 'Did I—er—mention that I might soon have nowhere to live?'

The grin that split Ryan's face was absolutely wonderful for her to see. 'You could try living with your husband, Mrs Carlisle,' he invited.

'I think,' Meredith replied a shade breathlessly, 'that I'd like to do that.'

His arms tightened about her, and again they kissed.

HARLEQUIN
Romance

Coming Next Month

#3043 MOUNTAIN LOVESONG Katherine Arthur
Lauren desperately needs help at her northern California holiday lodge, so
when John Smith, handyman *extraordinaire*, appears out of nowhere, he
seems the answer to her prayers. The only question—how long can she depend
on him?

#3044 SWEET ILLUSION Angela Carson
Dr. Luke Challoner, arrogant and domineering, expects everyone to bow to his
will. He is also one of the most attractive men Marion has ever met—which
doesn't stop her from standing up for herself against him!

#3045 HEART OF THE SUN Bethany Campbell
Kimberly came home to Eureka Springs to nurse a broken heart. Alec
Shaughnessy came to examine Ozark myth and folklore. Both become
entangled in a web of mystery that threatens to confirm an old prophesy—that
the women in Kimberly's family might never love happily.

#3046 THAT CERTAIN YEARNING Claudia Jameson
Diane's heart goes out to vulnerable young Kirsty, but warning bells sound
when she meets Kirsty's dynamic and outspoken uncle, Nik Channing. Yet she
has to support Kirsty, even if it means facing up to her feelings . . . and to Nik.

#3047 FULLY INVOLVED Rebecca Winters
Fight fire with fire—that was how Gina Lindsay planned to win back her ex-
husband. Captain Grady Simpson's career as a firefighter had destroyed his
marriage to Gina three years earlier. But now she's returned to Salt Lake
City—a firefighter, too. . . .

#3048 A SONG IN THE WILDERNESS Lee Stafford
Amber is horrified when noted journalist Lucas Tremayne becomes writer-
in-residence at the university where she is secretary to the dean. For Luke
had played an overwhelming part in her teenage past—one that Amber prefers
stay hidden. . . .

Available in April wherever paperback books are sold, or through
Harlequin Reader Service:

In the U.S.
901 Fuhrmann Blvd.
P.O. Box 1397
Buffalo, N.Y. 14240-1397

In Canada
P.O. Box 603
Fort Erie, Ontario
L2A 5X3

Harlequin Superromance®

LET THE GOOD TIMES ROLL . . .

Add some Cajun spice to liven up your New Year's celebrations and join Superromance for a romantic tour of the rich Acadian marshlands and the legendary Louisiana bayous.

CAJUN MELODIES, starting in January 1990, is a three-book tribute to the fun-loving people who've enriched America by introducing us to crawfish étouffé and gumbo, zydeco music and the Saturday night party, the *fais-dodo*. And learn about loving, Cajun-style, as you meet the tall, dark, handsome men who win their ladies' hearts with a beautiful, haunting melody. . . .

Book One: *Julianne's Song*, January 1990
Book Two: *Catherine's Song*, February 1990
Book Three: *Jessica's Song*, March 1990

If you missed Superromance #386 • *Julianne's Song*, #391 • *Catherine's Song* or #397 • *Jessica's Song*, and would like to order it, send your name, address, and zip or postal code, along with a check or money order for $2.95, plus 75¢ postage and handling, payable to Harlequin Reader Service to:

In the U.S.
901 Fuhrmann Blvd.
P.O. Box 1325
Buffalo, N.Y. 14269

In Canada
P.O. Box 609
Fort Erie, Ontario
L2A 5X3

Please specify book title with your order.   SRCJ-1A

This April, don't miss Harlequin's new Award of
Excellence title from

elusive as the unicorn

*When Eve Eden discovered that Adam
Gardener, successful art entrepreneur, was
searching for the legendary English artist, The
Unicorn, she nervously shied away. The Unicorn's
true identity hit too close to home....*

*Besides, Eve was rattled by Adam's
mesmerizing presence, especially in the light
of the ridiculous coincidence of their names—
and his determination to take advantage of it!
But Eve was already engaged to marry her
longtime friend, Paul.*

*Yet Eve found herself troubled by the different
choices Adam and Paul presented. If only the
answer to her dilemma didn't keep eluding her....*

HP1258-1

HARLEQUIN
American Romance®

Live the

Rocky Mountain Magic

Become a part of the magical events at The Stanley Hotel in the Colorado Rockies, and be sure to catch its final act in April 1990 with #337 RETURN TO SUMMER by Emma Merritt.

Three women friends touched by magic find love in a very special way, the way of enchantment. Hayley Austin was gifted with a magic apple that gave her three wishes in BEST WISHES (#329). Nicki Chandler was visited by psychic visions in SIGHT UNSEEN (#333). Now travel into the past with Kate Douglas as she meets her soul mate in RETURN TO SUMMER #337.

ROCKY MOUNTAIN MAGIC—All it takes is an open heart.